stay a little longer

DAWN LANUZA

Andrews McMeel
PUBLISHING®

To #romanceclass,
for fighting the good fight.

what's too far said he
where you are said she

E. E. CUMMINGS

"Something has given my poor warm life
Into the hand of someone random
Who doesn't know what even yesterday I was."

RAINER MARIA RILKE

one

It had been a long ride. Elan had ridden a bus for hours to the small town of San Juan to get his car. Normally, he found public transportation troublesome, but the moment he saw his friend Jules opening the gate for him, he stopped feeling antsy. Not even a bit unsettled.

He was just thankful.

And pathetic, because that guy waiting by the door was obviously the reason why Jules suddenly left the city as fast as she could. That's how Elan's car ended up in this driveway. That's why he was here in this town.

How had he ended up on the outside, while she was here with someone else? Well, Elan knew he'd had it coming. He'd seen her every day for the last few years but never made a move.

"I'm so sorry." She started apologizing as soon as she spotted him crossing the street toward the gate. It was an impressive gate. It screamed, "Rich people live here; don't even think about robbing us."

"I was supposed to ask someone to drive it back for you, but I—"

"Honestly, Jules," Elan replied as she took a step toward him. "It's all right. We're still on vacation, remember? It's nice to get out of the city for a bit."

Lie. Having grown up in the city, Elan wasn't used to small towns. He and his friends had flown to Bali a couple of weeks ago, but he ended up feeling even more anxious. He needed his life to be on schedule, and sitting by the beach for hours, no matter how beautiful it was, only made him think of how much time was passing by.

"Well." Her eyes darted to the other guy waiting by the door. Elan followed her gaze and took in the other man— his competition, so to speak—but it looked like he'd already won.

The guy walked toward them with a small smile on his face. To be polite, Elan guessed. He knew that smile only too well. He'd used it on many occasions throughout his life.

The guy stopped, still a step away from Jules, and nodded at Elan. "Hey, man."

He nodded back. "Sorry. Was I early?"

It did look like they'd just gotten up—eyes glazed, hair messy, clothes wrinkled. But it was almost noon. Was that usual for small towns?

Jules finally spoke up: "Kip, this is Elan."

The guy nodded again, as if he recognized his name. He extended his hand, and Elan took it. "Sorry 'bout the car. We were going to take it back, but everything's just been hectic with the move."

Elan shook his head. "Don't worry about it."

Jules sighed, "I owe you so much, seriously. Have you had breakfast yet?"

Of course he had.

She checked her watch, rolled her eyes. "I meant lunch! We should get something ordered—"

"I'd love to, Jules," Elan interrupted. "But I actually need to get back today."

That wasn't a lie. He needed to get back because he had errands early tomorrow and he needed his car.

"Well," she took a deep breath. "Thank you so much for lending it to me again. I promise, whatever you want—name it—I'll make sure you get it."

Kip raised an eyebrow, hiding a knowing smile as he took a sip of coffee. She cleared her throat. "I mean, as long as it's reasonable."

Elan raised his hand to get the keys, and Jules obliged, dropping them squarely into his palm. He walked over to the car, giving her another look before opening the door.

"Wait!" he heard someone scream.

Elan looked around and saw a girl running out of the house, dragging a huge suitcase behind her.

She was looking at him, so she must have wanted him to wait for her.

He stood there, one hand on the door handle, mouth slightly agape, as she approached him.

The first thing he noticed was her lips. Bright and red and full. Then there was her hair, jet black and slightly unruly after the run. She was tall and quite intimidating, especially with her eyes covered by huge, dark sunglasses.

"I'm coming with you," she announced. Like this had been discussed. Like this was supposed to happen. Like he shouldn't say no.

He sucked in a breath, glancing back at Jules for an introduction or a confirmation, but the girl was already talking. "Excuse me. Hey you, sir, could you open up your trunk, please?"

Jules only smiled at him nervously. So Elan did what he did best: he put on a smile and agreed. He walked over and helped the girl with her suitcase.

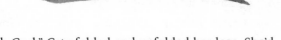

"Oh God." Caty folded and unfolded her legs. She'd been shifting in her seat for the last fifteen minutes. She felt uncomfortable sitting next to a guy she didn't know.

What was his name again? Last night they mentioned he was coming to pick up his Jeep. He was a classmate from law school or something. He didn't look like a lawyer or even someone who'd be one soon. She still found it weird that people her age could be called lawyers. For the longest time, she thought that was a job for old and boring men.

This guy did not look old at all. He looked like the kind of guy you saw in high school but didn't get to know because he liked to sit in a corner, all quiet and brooding. You wouldn't really notice him until the growth spurt finally kicked in. He would be the one who shocked everyone during the reunion, the little underdog. He just had that look about him. He was attractive but obviously didn't know how much or didn't care to inquire. He also had the most interesting nose—slightly crooked on the bridge, like it was broken in a brawl or a tackle. It gave the impression that he was more dangerous than he intended.

Yet he had his shirt all tucked in, hair coiffed neatly. He looked like the nicest boy in town.

Only he hadn't looked at her since he started driving, and he hadn't said one word. She wasn't sure if he was shy or just unapproachable.

This was the most uncomfortable drive she'd ever been on, and that included the ride she once shared with a woman whom an ex-boyfriend was currently seeing. *With the ex-boyfriend in the same car.*

She cleared her throat, assessing her situation: she was about to fly back to Toronto. Her parents had just sold her childhood home, and she didn't want to be too emotional about it. After all, San Juan wasn't her home anymore. She'd been away since moving to Toronto about a decade ago.

"So, you're Juliana's friend, right?" Caty started, figuring that he wouldn't talk unless she did.

He paused. "Yeah, Jules."

Jules. How chummy. She'd been a friend of Juliana's since they were babies, but she was never just *Jules.*

"Thanks for giving me a ride, by the way," she said, getting that out of the way. "I'm glad to finally get out of there, you know?"

His eyebrows furrowed.

She felt the need to explain. "Not that it isn't great. It is. My brother and my best friend. *Together.* That's, like, a porn story line."

He swerved right about the time she said that last bit, and it was too funny to watch him try to recover. He let out a nervous laugh and bit his lip as if to stop himself from showing emotion.

It would have worked, she thought, if it were someone else she knew better. It was an icebreaker of sorts, a funny ha-ha comment that should have relieved the awkwardness. But not with a complete stranger, and not in the Philippines, where sex was not something you talked about with a person you've only just met. Also, *porn* was definitely a taboo word.

Great, she'd made it more awkward.

Caty looked away, wincing at herself. "Sorry, wrong thing to say."

She didn't see how he reacted, didn't even hear a response. She thought there was still some time left before they reached their destination, and the silence was starting to annoy her. It would have helped if there were music in the background, but the radio wasn't on either. It was just so . . . quiet.

Caty glanced at him. "Well, we're stuck together now. We have to talk about something."

"And porn's the first thing that came to mind?"

Her eyes slanted. "Like sex isn't something you think about."

He licked his lower lip and bit back a smile.

Really, what did she have to do to make this guy even grin? She frowned and itched to ask him why he was so poor at handing out smiles and eye contact. Granted, they were strangers, but they were currently sharing a space and could at least be polite.

But maybe he already was being polite to her. She had asked him for a favor by giving her a ride.

Caty decided to pull back. "I didn't mean like you give off a creepy vibe. You don't. We can just talk about, I don't know, how old this car is."

He snorted as soon as the word *old* left her mouth.

All right, Caty thought. *This guy is stuck-up. He couldn't possibly have been offended by that.* She was just really curious. Her father had taught her to like cars, and she knew the older ones often had interesting histories.

She clicked her tongue and took off her sunglasses, his silence starting to make her feel bad about what she'd just said, even though she hadn't meant for it to come off that way. She racked her brain for something else to say, but really, he should be the one to break the silence so she could stop saying the wrong things.

Yet he just sat there, focused on the road. *This guy can't be so boring,* Caty thought. *After all, he's Juliana's friend.* From what she could gather, Juliana liked him, but they didn't date or fool around.

That's Juliana. She was mostly anti–fooling around, even when they were kids. She liked rules and wanted things to be in order.

Caty tried again. "Okay, you can pick the topic. I'll bite."

She sensed his hesitation. His arms stiffened as he squeezed the steering wheel. If he hadn't been so focused on being uninterested in socializing, she would have thought he was really cute.

Then, "Fine. I suppose you can tell me about your childhood."

She paused. "Wow."

"Wow?"

"Wow," Caty repeated. "That's very first date-y. Or not even. At least the third date."

"You have to wait for a third date to talk about your childhood?"

"Yeah," Caty nodded. "Third date's the time to decide if you're gonna keep seeing the dude. He passed the impression test on the first date, and let's face it, the second one is a do-over. Just to make sure he's really cute without the beer goggles on."

She slowed down, watching his reaction. His eyebrows raised then knitted. He didn't smile, but *boy* did his eyes talk.

"Beer goggles," he repeated, saying that a little bit slower. "What kind of first dates have you been having?"

"Fun ones," she replied. "And don't judge, *Judy*."

He snorted. *He thinks that's funny?* But it was a reaction, finally.

"So what do you talk about on first dates?" He finally glanced at her, eyes slowly scanning her face before turning back. Then he did a peculiar thing: sort of shuddered and made it look like he was clearing his throat.

"Oh," Caty cooed. "Why? Is this a first date?"

"No, no," he said, as if that was a silly idea. "I'm just asking since you were so against talking about your childhood."

"I'm not against it," Caty shrugged. "I'm just saying. Those are things you don't ask people right off the bat."

"But asking them if they've seen porn is?"

She widened her eyes. *Now there he is.* She's getting warmer. He's starting to show some personality, doing more than simply shaking his head, crossing his eyebrows, or snorting at her.

"Hey, I didn't ask. I just said," she clarified. "Everybody's seen porn. I absolutely won't believe it if you say you haven't."

"I didn't," he said. Was that a shadow of a smile on his lips?

Caty kept her eyes on him. "What's your name again?"

The smile on his lips finally formed. It was reserved and polite but a smile, still. "Elan."

"I'm Caty, by the way. In case you've forgotten by now and are too scared to ask again."

"I haven't," he snapped.

Caty leaned back. "Elan, huh? Where did that come from?"

"The dictionary," he answered flatly. So he was funny, after all. Caty felt herself smiling triumphantly for having coaxed a joke out of his polite-to-the-point-of-stuck-up exterior. "It's French. I think it means *enthusiasm* or something like that."

"Are you French?"

"Non," he answered.

"Ah, parlez-vous français?"

He paused. "I've been asked that question more than once, and sometimes I say, 'Oui,' and then I take it back."

"You shouldn't. You should keep faking it."

He shook his head. "I don't know any other French words."

"I can teach you," Caty offered. Sure, they only had a little time left, and they'd just met, but she could teach him a thing or two.

"You speak French?"

"A little bit. It was an elective at school. Not that I paid much attention. I visited Montreal a couple of times and learned the language better."

"So I take it you actually knew what my name meant?"

"Well," she answered, "no. I only speak tourist. I don't think élan is used in everyday conversations."

"Oh."

"I can teach you how to say important phrases, though."

"Like?"

"Voulez-vous coucher—"

"All right," he cut her off. "I know what that means."

Caty cackled, "Good. I was testing you."

Elan gave her a look—one eyebrow arched—and something struck her about what he was doing. If he wasn't too careful, someone might confuse it with calculated seduction.

He couldn't be flirting with her, could he? That would be a weird turnaround of events considering how they started. They had been stumbling so bad and were just starting to find a rhythm.

"Je m'en fous," Caty coughed.

"What does that mean?"

"You have to say it first. Je m'en fous."

He pressed his lips together as if he was thinking about making an excuse not to do it, but he failed.

Caty laughed. "You don't have to look constipated. The French language is very sexy."

"And complicated. It's never spoken how it's spelled."

She rolled her eyes. "You don't seem to have a lot of élan today, Elan."

"Well," he sighed, "it's a tough name to live up to."

She laughed, more like a cackle. He was *really* funny, she decided, and she was finally starting to enjoy the ride.

"What about your name? Where did it come from?"

"Catalina," Caty answered with a wince. "Nothing special. My parents liked naming their kids after ancestors."

"It's also the name of a saint," he pointed out.

"I heard."

"She was a martyr."

Caty took a deep breath and sighed. "Well, look at that. We're both saddled with names we can't possibly live up to."

Elan threw her a glance, and she offered a quick smile.

"This is good." Caty nodded mostly to herself, adjusting her position on the seat. "Talking about the origins of our names, I'll keep it in mind as good first-date material."

"You get a lot of first dates?"

She found his question funny. "Sure. Don't you?"

"Not really."

Ah. Caty felt smug. So her theory about Elan not being the most popular person in school might be true. "I get why you're friends with Juliana now."

two

Did he actually *shudder?*

He had. He'd looked into her eyes and shuddered. He almost cursed but managed to clear his throat.

She had an air of confidence. He'd seen that as soon as she ran from the house to his car, and who could blame her? She was attractive, and she probably knew it, had probably played her looks to her advantage for most of her life.

But her eyes were a different story. She was doe-eyed, looking at him with sincere interest—or at least he thought. Whether or not it was true, he thought she really had the most beautiful, expressive eyes.

Then she laughed, which broke the image he had of her the first time they met. Granted, that was only minutes ago, but it felt like she was starting to unravel.

She said she was Jules's best friend, which did not make sense. For as long as he'd known her, Jules had been quiet and mysterious. It was like the freaking Great Wall of China surrounded her. She was sealed and airtight. So that dude she was with earlier? He must have torn down that wall.

When Caty had said the word *friends,* it clung to him like a terrifying leech sucking on his back. He wouldn't mind if it came from somebody else, but somehow this girl made his friendship with Jules a terrible thing.

He let out a nervous chuckle, "Really."

"Yeah," she exclaimed, "Plato's a genius, you know?"

Elan continued driving, shaking his head as he let Caty explain the whole thing. He'd read Plato before and thought it was quite silly. See, according to Plato, once upon a time, people were born with four arms, four legs, and two heads. Elan hadn't taken it seriously when he read it, even less so when he heard it from someone else.

"Now, thanks to Zeus, we've all been separated. Now we only have two hands, two feet, and a head."

"I don't see why the separation bums you out. I'm not sure how I'd feel having two heads."

"Oh, you should definitely know." She squinted, gave him a knowing smirk before he got it. He reacted too late so she just carried on. "Anyway, are you serious? We're walking halves! We've been split in two."

She paused for a minute, as if thinking of what she'd said. He could imagine there were a lot of thoughts swirling around in her head that she was holding back. In the end, she shrugged, "Classic Zeus, always ruining lives."

He laughed at that. How fast she jumped from one thought to another.

"What does this myth have to do with Jules being my friend?" Elan asked.

"Well," Caty gave him a look, as if giving him a final check before saying, "You are kind of like her. She could be your other half."

It wasn't the first time he'd heard that. People joked that Jules was his twin or his sister just because they got along so well. In the years they'd known each other, there had been very little conflict.

Elan shrugged. "I guess."

"You sure you're not hiding any feelings for her?"

He had been asked about this too many times—by his mother, his sister, people at school who dared to ask. And himself, at night sometimes, when he allowed his mind to wonder.

He frowned, lips pouting a bit. "I don't know."

"You don't know?"

He turned to her and blinked slowly. This was the look he gave people that usually made them stop bugging him, but he had the impression that it was not gonna work on her.

She simply grinned at him, so he turned his eyes back to the road.

"Hmm," he heard her say. "Interesting."

"It's not a yes."

"It's not a no, either."

She had a point. But then again, there was that guy standing by the doorway earlier today, Caty's brother. "What does it matter anyway? She's clearly with your brother."

"Well, duh, they're totally doing it," Caty said flat out.

Elan flinched, surprised at how those words stung. "Well, I didn't need to know that."

"Doesn't mean it's not true," Caty insisted.

He shook his head.

A wicked smile appeared on her lips. "It's not just that. I'm sure they're in *love* or something. They spend a ridiculous amount of time staring at each other, and the sexual tension is so thick around the house. I had to get out. Fast."

Elan cleared his throat. He was curious, even though he knew he should stop asking.

"Pretty sure I was cock blocking the entire time," she added, giving him more visuals he didn't need.

He almost hit the brakes then. He really did. But there was a car behind them, and he could only deal with one problem at a time.

Caty smiled, a little bit coy. "You mad, Judy?"

"No," he answered, breathing out his nose.

"Sure?"

He smirked and shook his head.

"Don't worry. You're not the first one. Everyone's a little bit in love with Jules. She's perfect. She's smart."

"Jealous?"

She smiled, slowly and mischievously. "I don't get jealous."

Elan didn't believe her. She looked like it, sounded like it too. Some friend this must be.

"We have a complicated relationship," she told him. "But she is my oldest friend, and I am loyal to her."

He wondered how much longer they had to keep talking. He hoped she would fall asleep just so he could concentrate. He liked to drive in silence—it was therapeutic. He solved problems during this time, and the roads were a cathartic way for him to undo the knots in his head.

"Can you take a turn over there?" She pointed to the right.

Elan's eyes followed, "Why?"

"You can drop me off there, actually."

"I thought you needed a ride to the airport."

"I do," she answered, "but I actually made plans with my friend. He's taking me instead. I just really needed to get out of the house."

Then why the hell did she tell Jules he was going to take her? He wanted to say that out loud but held back.

"It's not too far away," she assured him. "I'll get out of your hair in about five minutes. Then you can go back to your life."

She pointed, "Just turn right here."

It was a village gate, one with security guards manning the front. To be honest, Elan was relieved that he didn't have to drive her all the way to the airport, but he was a bit worried as well. He knew Juliana would ask about the ride. How would she feel if he just dropped off her childhood friend at some unknown place?

They stopped at the gate, and a guard approached. Elan rolled the window down, and Caty leaned forward.

"Diaz," she said. The guard seemed to recognize her and merely took a look at Elan's driver's license before waving them through.

She was quiet on the way in, like she had been switched off or run out of battery power. "Take another right."

Elan followed her directions until they reached a two-story house sitting in a huge lot.

"Park right here."

The house looked like it had been built awhile ago, but it was well maintained. In the short time he'd spent in town, he'd gotten the impression that really wealthy people lived there. Not new-money kind of rich but old-family rich. Generations of wealthy families preserving their Spanish Colonial-era houses and impressive, intimidating gates.

"So this is your friend's?" he asked.

"Yeah," she agreed, "something like that."

She opened her door, and Elan started to get out, but she stopped him. "Don't worry, I'll get my bag. Just open the trunk."

"Don't be silly."

"No, really." Caty touched his arm and squeezed lightly, leaning closer to him. He could smell her then, and the scent reminded him of ylang-ylang. It was subtly sweet with a hint of spice, but she pulled away before he could be sure. "Thanks for the ride, Judy."

"Sure." Elan would have reacted to her calling him Judy, but he saw the change in her demeanor. She was tense and seemed a bit scared. His eyes searched for hers, but she leaped out, grabbed her bag, and stood on the sidewalk for a second.

He let the motor idle and watched as she approached the gate. She seemed surprised he was still there, so she waved him away. He was determined to stay, at least until he was sure he'd dropped her off at the right place.

No one was opening the gate, so he thought he could help by honking the horn, and a loud beep blurted out.

Eyes wide, Caty left her bag on the sidewalk and walked over to the car with a murderous look on her face.

"Just. Go," she mouthed.

Unbelievable, he shook his head. How could she be so annoyed when he was trying to do something helpful. So he just did what he'd been wanting to do since they left Jules and Kip— he drove away.

Slowly, but away.

She shouldn't be here. She knew that. But she just had to see for herself.

Maybe it was a curse her parents had named her Catalina, after all. She hadn't thought about it until Elan mentioned the saint's martyrdom. She was a martyr for standing outside this house when she knew she shouldn't.

But what she knew didn't change what she felt.

Caty hated coming back to San Juan. People seemed welcoming, but she knew better. They liked to talk here, dig out secrets and taunt each other with smug smiles, winks, and passive-aggressive comments.

With everything that had happened to Caty before she left for Toronto, she was pretty sure that people *knew* her so-called secrets. She had been terrified that someday people would so casually mention these at gatherings, like it was one of those town anecdotes.

Back then, she'd found a distraction in Otto—the very person who was now peeking out from a window. Right now, she was hoping he could still do the same.

Caty raised her hand, but he disappeared. She turned back to her phone and reviewed the unanswered messages she'd sent him. Out of the corner of her eye, Caty saw Elan's car slowly driving away. Then she looked up and, to her surprise, found someone else stepping out of the house. *Madeline, who was not supposed to be there!* She was supposed to be on a trip, at least that's what Otto had told Caty.

For a moment, she stood frozen on the sidewalk. Only when Madeline approached the gate did Caty find herself frantically pulling at her luggage.

Ah, shit. She let go of the suitcase and saw that Elan's car was about to turn the corner. *No, no, no.*

Caty waved her hands and screamed to get his attention. She knew she'd told him to go, but, *Please, God, please make him turn around.* She heard someone else shout—it was Otto, she was sure of it—but she didn't have time to look back.

She thought, *I'm being chased by Otto's fiancé. This is real. This is happening.*

"Elan!" Caty shouted, running as fast as she could.

To her relief, the car stopped. She screamed his name one more time, and he reversed, stopping just in time for her to open the door and jump in as if they were in a bank heist.

He was her getaway car.

"Go, go, go, drive!"

When she was safe inside the car, Caty finally turned and saw a glimpse of Otto. She'd seen him earlier this year when she came back for a visit. They had met and reconnected. Madeline wasn't even in the picture then. She was just the new "girlfriend of the month," but now she had a boulder of a diamond flashing on her ring finger. Caty hadn't missed that.

She had met Otto when she was young and he was, well, older. He was her father's friend—the cool guy who dropped by their house to talk about cars and sometimes business. Her father showed him how to restore cars while her brother, Kip, watched and she stayed in her room.

Over the years, Otto was the one who never seemed to marry. He just had occasional girlfriends—all gorgeous, all younger. Madeline was even younger than Caty. Everyone knew her as that kid that Sarge Reynoso, the local TV celebrity, mentored. She took acting and dance classes with him and was determined to be a big star. She had a few successes but never had her big break, so she decided she'd rather be a big fish in a small pond.

Madeline sure caught a big fish, because Otto was the biggest catch of all. He was the Resident Bachelor, and since coming home, all Caty'd heard from the gossips was how Madeline finally got Otto to settle down.

But Caty had thought Otto would leave Madeline. She was only supposed to last for a month, maybe a couple more.

Stupid, stupid, stupid.

Caty really shouldn't be with someone like Otto. She knew that. He'd told her so. Even gave her all the reasons.

For one thing, it would be a long-distance relationship since she was in Toronto. She didn't believe in that. She couldn't survive on pining. Caty needed the comfort of having the person there—the security, the companionship.

But Otto was a grown-up, she reasoned. He could do anything. Except break up with Madeline. Except meet her and at least tell her why he had chosen the other woman over her.

Caty turned away and covered her face for a minute, feeling the heat on her cheeks from running, and maybe a little bit because of the disgrace. She looked up and felt Elan watching her. She dared to look directly at him, but he dodged it. He had one hand over his mouth, as if he was deciding whether to let her stay or kick her out.

She sat back in her seat and decided to stay quiet.

They drove in silence until Elan suddenly pulled over to the side of the road. He rolled the window down and rested one hand on the steering wheel. He took a deep breath, shoulders lifting as he did, then bowed his head and muttered under his breath.

She watched him for a moment until he seemed to calm down.

When Elan finally turned back to her, Caty realized she'd been holding her breath the entire time. She exhaled slowly, watching him watch her.

She took another breath, then asked, "Were you counting Mississippis?"

"No," he spat. "Yes."

"Why?"

"Because—" he paused. "Hang on. I'm supposed to be the one asking questions. How about you tell me what the hell happened back there?"

Caty felt herself close off as shame flooded over her. Was she still trying to win over an engaged man? She didn't know what she was doing; she only knew that she needed to run away and be somewhere else. But she didn't live in San Juan anymore, so she had nowhere else to go but to the only person she still knew, Otto.

She felt like crawling into the back of the vehicle. "Nothing. I don't want to talk about it."

"You're not even gonna tell me who those people are?"

Caty blinked at him, arms crossed over her chest. She looked away, her legs crossed, and her face completely hidden by her hair. How could she actually tell him without being judged? She knew she shouldn't have gone to the house, but apparently she was too stubborn for her own good.

Scratch that, she was too lonely. She needed the distraction.

"Jesus Christ," Elan spat out. "At least tell me what I'm getting into by sticking with you."

There was so much frustration in his voice that she had to look. He seemed rattled, and he took another deep breath, exhaling through his mouth, fighting to keep himself calm.

Shit, Caty thought, recognizing those expressions.

Elan licked his lips and turned back to the steering wheel. Without another word, he started driving. It seemed too late to say anything more, so she didn't. She simply watched him drive in silence.

All the rapport they'd been building was gone, she thought. They actually had something going on earlier; they were getting warm and gaining momentum.

"Where are we going?" she finally asked.

Silence. *Fantastic.* Now he's back to ignoring her. Caty hated it when her questions weren't answered, but that's what she'd done to him earlier, and now she was getting a dose of her own medicine.

She marveled at how she could make herself feel even more alone by simply looking for company. So Caty simply closed her eyes and hummed a song to herself until she fell asleep.

three

They arrived at the airport. Only . . .

Caty bit her lip since Elan was still ignoring her. He did wake her up to tell her they were at the airport, but not a word more.

So what did he want from her? He wanted to know what the hell happened earlier. She got chased by Otto and Madeline, that's what. Did he need to know why? Absolutely not.

For one thing, he's a Judy. Second, he's Juliana's friend, which makes him Double Judy.

"Do you need help with anything?" he asked.

"No," she answered, fumbling around her seat, not sure what she needed to do first. She had just woken up. Her head was still a bit woozy, her hair was a mess, and she needed a splash of water on her face.

"I'm not flying out yet," she said.

He froze. His entire body went rigid.

"I lied. I told Juliana I moved my flight so I could get out of the house. As I said, sexual tension. Thick," Caty explained. "I fly out tomorrow morning."

Elan tilted his head slightly. His jaw twitched, as if to say, *So now what?*

"Can you please take me to a nearby hotel instead?"

He took a moment before he nodded, exhaled heavily, and drove out of the departure lane.

It was killing Caty that he kept ignoring her. She didn't like it. She didn't know him, but she hated being ignored. Usually it was okay if someone didn't like her, but him? He just seemed utterly disappointed. Or let down. She didn't understand why, and she couldn't let it go.

"I wasn't welcome in that house," Caty said quickly, looking away. She didn't want to see his expression as she tried to explain. "Obviously, I didn't know how much, but now I do."

Still nothing. Caty stole a quick glance at Elan, but he was still doing his best to avoid her. It was as if he was on autopilot, driving her to her next destination.

"Elan," she called his name.

His jaw twitched, but he stayed focused on driving. Caty exhaled loudly, letting him know she was tired of the silent treatment. When they got to the hotel nearest to the airport—the one with the expensive shops and casino—Caty pointed out, "I can't afford this."

He winced, shook his head, and drove away to find another hotel. They found one, all right, but it was still not in her price range.

"I didn't pay my credit card bill last month," Caty said aloud, so Elan had to drive away again.

They ended up at one of those budget places, the kind you stay in just to sleep and do nothing else. It was still near the airport, so she could ask the concierge to get her a cab when it was actually time for her to fly out.

She didn't protest when he parked. She followed him to the reception area and nodded when he asked, "A standard room okay with you?"

He reached for his wallet, but she touched his elbow. She felt the jolt when he flinched. "What are you doing? I'm paying for it; that's why I kept telling you to stop going to the expensive ones."

Elan finally met her eyes, and she was glad to see there was some life in them at least. He didn't look as resigned anymore. Caty fished out her wallet and handed her credit card to the receptionist, who wore a gold nameplate that said *Diane*.

They kept quiet until Diane checked Caty in and handed her the room keys. "No luggage?" she asked.

Not anymore, Caty thought. Then she remembered her favorite sweater was in the suitcase and silently cursed. "No. Thank you."

Despite her lack of luggage, a bellboy led them up to the elevators and pressed four. Not a word was uttered inside the metal box. Caty almost felt apologetic that the bellboy was stuck in the middle of this Elan snowstorm.

When the doors opened, she heaved a sigh. The rest was pretty quick and standard. The bellboy opened the room and told them to enjoy their stay. Caty stepped inside and threw her purse on the bed while Elan looked around the room.

"Not too bad," she finally said.

Elan just replied, "It's all right."

Caty sat on the bed, her feet crossed and hands tucked in her belly. She didn't say anything for a while, just watched Elan stand awkwardly near the door. She was waiting for him to tell her what he'd been meaning to say hours ago.

Instead he turned to her and asked, "Are you gonna be okay?"

Her eyes lifted up to him, her shock apparent. That wasn't the first thing she thought he'd ask, but it was way better than what she was expecting. She smiled weakly, "I guess."

"Okay, good."

"Have you stayed here before?" she asked.

"No."

She nodded, and the silence returned.

"So I should go," Elan finally said. It seemed to bounce off the walls.

She knew she should say "I know" or "thank you," but instead it came out, "I don't mind if you stay."

She sensed a reaction, but it was polite. That was his gig. He was performing the shit out of it today. "No, thank you. I really should go."

"You said you were going to drive me to the airport," Caty pointed out.

"I did," Elan answered, as if he'd just remembered that.

"But what about later?"

"I can talk to the front desk; they'll get a cab for you."

"But you told Juliana you'd take me," she insisted. There was no point to this; she was just making him talk. For what? To make her feel better at least, to give her time to leave him with a nicer impression of her.

"Yes, but that was when you told me you were flying out today."

"So I lied," she scoffed.

Elan put his hands in his pockets and laughed, "What are you doing?"

She looked up at him innocently.

"You're stalling me," he said, very matter-of-factly.

Caty stared. That was new—a different Elan. That wasn't so polite and nice. "You were secretly hoping you'd take Juliana home with you, right?"

She watched Elan turn pale. She gave herself a pat on the back, not for making him look bad but for throwing something out there and being right about it.

"Well . . . yeah," he said.

"She didn't tell you about my brother?"

Elan took a deep breath. "We don't talk about things like that."

Caty smiled. "My brother is quick. He grabs life by the balls. If he sees something he wants, he just goes for it."

Elan's brows met in the middle, but he resorted to a shrug.

Caty finally stood up from the bed and walked toward him. "Really? That's how you react? You just shrug it off?"

He took his hands out of his pockets, starting to turn away. "This is not gonna work, Caty. You won't get a reaction from me about this."

She hesitated, then tapped his arm so he wouldn't walk away. Elan turned to her, and she pushed herself up on tiptoes, grabbed him by the nape, and kissed him.

This always seemed to do the trick. Why not try it now?

There were plenty of ways to get out of something. Fake an emergency. Pretend to be sick. Be a fucking adult and tell the truth.

But did he want to?

Elan felt Caty draw away and then realized how they were linked. His hands were grabbing her forearms. She had her hands in his hair. Their lips had been locked just a second ago.

How the hell?

"Lunch?" Caty disentangled herself from him.

"What?" was all he could get out. Everything was suddenly hazy, and all he could see was Caty running back to the bed to get her purse.

"Come on. It's the least I could do for giving me a ride."

He could still taste her lips on his. It was sweet but subtle, much like her scent.

"Elan," she called again, one hand resting on the door handle.

His legs dragged as he followed her down the hallway. He blinked a couple of times, wondering why and how he was still here with her. Wasn't he supposed to have left her by now?

Caty threw him a glance, and his eyes dropped to her lips. They looked the same as the first time he saw her, but now his mouth was filled with how they tasted, and he wanted more.

They stopped by the elevator. Caty pressed the button before turning back to him. "You okay?"

"Yeah." He looked at her, focusing on her eyes, her hair, *anywhere* but her lips. Her forehead, he could focus on that instead.

Ah, shit, Elan thought. Is this happening? Is this what it's going to be like now? Wasn't she the same girl he was ignoring an hour ago?

He didn't like what had happened at her friend's house earlier. He wasn't a fan of situations that involved chasing and running and trouble. He told himself he was studying law to bring some order in the world. To create a better sense of peace. Yet here he was, standing in front of a girl, and all he could think of was, *I'm in trouble.*

She smiled, her lips spreading wide. "Are you thinking about it?"

His eyes shot up to her. "No. What?"

"The buffet, man," Caty answered, like it was the most obvious thing. Beside her, there was a poster announcing buffet hours at the restaurant next door.

"No. I'm not."

"Well, I am." She shrugged. Right then, the elevator door opened, and he was thankful she had turned around.

Elan stepped inside, putting an acceptable distance between the two of them. He asked himself again how it had happened. One minute they were having a spat and the next they were kissing. Or she was kissing him. He was simply responding.

Fine, he kissed her back. He was sure of that. He had been kissed unexpectedly before and simply didn't return it, ducked away, and told the girl she had the wrong idea.

This one was hard to avoid, and she knew just what she was doing.

Caty swayed, more cheerful than before the kiss. Her fingers touched his momentarily but didn't linger. He watched her from the corner of his eye as she smiled at her reflection on the elevator.

He ran a hand across his nape, extremely aware that his skin was still tingling from the memory of her hands.

The doors opened, and they got out.

Thank Christ.

The huge clock on the wall showed that it was way past lunch hour. Elan caught up with Caty as she exited the hotel and entered the restaurant next door. A waiter welcomed them and started leading them to a table, but Caty told him she'd rather stay at the bar.

She sat on a stool, and he simply followed, still at a loss for words as things spiraled out of his control. She ordered a rum and coke and a glass of water, then threw him a questioning look.

Elan replied, "Gin and tonic."

Caty snorted, "Sorry, but a friend told me gin and tonic is for old men."

"And rum and coke?"

"College girls who never outgrew it."

Just then the bartender handed her a glass of water, and she raised it to Elan. "Cheers, Grandpa."

He rubbed a hand over his nape again, then over his hair to fix it. It was longer than his usual cut, and he had the vacation as an excuse for avoiding a trip to the barber.

"I always thought gin and tonic was the classy choice," he admitted, "but yeah, it's an old man's drink. I got it from my uncle."

His "uncle" was also a lawyer. They weren't related by blood, but Pascual was his childhood hero. Like Superman, Pascual swooped in when Elan's family needed help. Now Elan worked for his firm while he waited for the bar exam results. He was always encouraging him to take a break, but Elan kept coming back for more things to do anyway.

Caty raised her eyebrows as she sipped. "So what's your real drink?"

He shrugged. He didn't really have one. He wasn't much of a drinker. "I don't know. Just beer."

"Beer is cool. It's not pretentious. It's simple." Caty set her glass down. "Next time, just get beer."

Next time.

The bartender handed Caty her rum and coke, and Elan suggested, "We should get something to eat too."

"Right," she nodded. "Lunch, that's what I said. Not drinks. But we could use it. You more than me."

"Hmm? The food or the drinks?"

"Both. You looked a bit dazed a second ago."

"Well, yeah," Elan jumped. He was going to be frank because they weren't children. If he was going to stay until she left, he didn't want to stare at her lips the whole time. He was aware that he was doing it again. "You kissed me."

Caty nodded, "I did."

"And?" he stalled. "That's what we do now?"

"You've never just kissed anyone before?" She took the first gulp of her drink.

No, he thought. *But yes*. Maybe when he was younger. Did he?

"It took you awhile to answer, so you probably haven't," she assumed.

"You're right, I probably haven't."

"Did you like it?" she teased.

He didn't know what to say. She was waiting for him to answer with no trace of regret or embarrassment on her face. What should he say? *Yes? No?* The latter would just be cruel and a plain lie.

Elan could see the line, and his toes were on the edge of it. Only he wasn't sure if he was already on the other side after that kiss.

"But you've kissed girls before, right?"

Elan gave her a look.

"Boys?"

He sighed, exasperated. "Yes, I have kissed girls before."

"I'm just kidding; I knew that. You knew what you were doing. I just didn't know which way you swing." She laughed, handing him a menu.

"I'm not gay," he clarified.

"Nothing wrong with it."

"I didn't say—" Elan exhaled.

Caty cut him off with a laugh, "It doesn't take much to annoy you."

That wasn't him. He always tried to be calm and collected. "No, especially when you enjoy doing it."

She nodded, eyes focused on the menu. "That's true."

"Why?"

She ordered a full meal, roast chicken or something, before she answered, "Because. When you're annoyed, you're not such a dud. And I enjoy Angry Elan's company more."

Elan straightened his back and insisted, "I'm not angry."

She rolled her eyes at him.

He didn't say anything else. It was her opinion, and he wouldn't argue. He could live with that. Maybe.

"Can you relax, please?" She started again. "It's not like I'm assessing you for something. I don't have to go back to Jules and give a rave review of your services for the day."

"Services?"

"You know what I mean. You did this nice thing for me, so you're keeping up with the image. I get it. But quit it."

"You want me to be mean to you?"

She shook her head fast. "Not mean. Real. Come to think of it, we're actually the best kind of strangers."

"In what way?"

She swiveled her seat to face him. "In the way that I'll be halfway around the world in a matter of hours. We never have to see each other again."

Elan shook his head. "No, we have people in common. We're not total strangers."

"Do we really?" She squinted her eyes.

The way she said it gave him the impression that they didn't, and he remembered she'd said that her relationship with Jules was complicated. Maybe they weren't really friends in the best sense of the word. And maybe she was the type who appeared every once in a while then disappeared off the face of the earth. A one-time thing, a rare occurrence, like a comet.

"What makes that perfect?"

"We can stop being the people we think we should be and just . . . be." Caty lifted the glass of gin and tonic and handed it to him. "Do you get me?"

He did. It made sense. He took the glass. "So you're telling me we should just be honest with each other?"

She leaned back in her chair. "I don't know about you, Judy, but I've been honest with you since I got in your car."

"Except when you didn't tell me why you were being chased by someone at that house."

She sighed, a loud one, and dropped her shoulders. "You're still not over that?"

"It was just hours ago," Elan insisted. "Why weren't you welcome? Whose house was it anyway?"

She remained slumped in her seat. "Okay. Fine. I was specifically told not to go there."

"Because?"

"Hold on," she said, raising a finger. "Let's make this fun. You ask me a question, I answer. I ask you a question, you answer."

"And if one of us refuses?"

Her face crumpled. "Why would you even do that? Don't spoil the fun."

"I'm just saying." Elan finally took a sip and let the sensation of the liquid linger. "So we have options."

She snapped her fingers. "Okay. If you refuse to answer, you have to do something for me and vice versa."

"So it's like Truth or Dare?" He frowned.

"*Oh, Elan, you're so fun!* That's what all the girls say."

"Okay, fine."

Caty put her drink down and clapped her hands. "I've got a good one."

"I'm sure." He stared at the ceiling, cursing himself for agreeing to this.

"How'd you get the nose?"

Elan felt his body jerk. *His nose?* He touched the slightly crooked bridge. He'd lived a part of his life with a straight nose, just like his mother's until . . . "Basketball."

"You play basketball?"

He pointed at her. "Not your turn. Why weren't you welcome?"

She rolled her eyes. "Because someone else is already living there, aside from my friend."

"But why would she chase—"

She held out a hand to stop him from asking a question out of turn. "You play basketball?"

A plate of pork chops was laid out in front of him, hot and fresh from the grill.

He didn't really play basketball, but she hadn't said anything about lying in the game. He just had to say something so he could get to his questions. "Yes. Not well, but yes."

"I can't see it."

"What do you think I play?"

"I don't know, bridge, chess, snakes and ladders." She flashed him a patronizing smile, and he returned it with his middle finger.

Caty's face lit up. "My friend Angry Elan is back." She grabbed his face with both hands and pinched his cheeks.

Elan batted her hands away. "Your turn."

But she wasn't done. "I expected a story. You know, I've been making up stories about your nose since we met. Bar fight over a girl. A girl punching you in the face after you broke up with her. Tell me if I'm getting warm."

"Basketball."

Caty shook her head. "So you just got elbowed by some other dude?"

"Yeah."

"You should use one of my stories."

"Is that what you do?" Wait, that wasn't supposed to be his next question.

"No. I'm a stylist."

"Meaning?"

She raised her hand. "You'll get your turn. What's the first thing you noticed about me?"

Her lips. Did she really ask him that, and did it mean the first thing she noticed about him was his crooked nose? It was the wrong, imperfect part of him.

"Your hair," he settled. Really, it wasn't just her lips; it was everything. *She had color,* whatever that meant. That's what he thought when he first saw her. That, and her full, red lips. He really had to stop going on and on about them.

She tucked a strand of hair under her ear, as if that answer satisfied her. He never understood what women wanted to hear when they asked questions like that. She seemed pleased with his answer, so he patted himself on the back.

"Stylist?" Elan continued.

"Yeah. Prop styling."

He gave her a quizzical look.

"It's just a fancy name for putting pretty things together. I took interior design, but I think I'm more comfortable with smaller spaces. I can manage them better."

"Things as in?" was all he said.

"Products. To sell," she explained. "It's like doing a window display, but now it's for your teeny-tiny mobile screens. Times are changing, Grandpa."

"Got it," he said, impressed. "Wow."

"You didn't even ask me if I'm good at it."

Elan gave in to her demand. "Should I?"

"Do you think I am?"

He cleared his throat. Here it goes again. Putting him on the hot seat. Elan looked at her face, still radiating the confidence he had picked up the moment they met. "Well, you seem as if you know how to put pretty things together," he gestured at her.

"Are you telling me I look pretty?"

Elan sputtered, "Sure."

Caty beamed at him. "And the first thing you noticed about me is my hair? You missed my face or something?"

He smiled but looked away. "I don't think it's your turn to ask a question anymore."

"Yeah, but we messed the whole thing up."

"We should just stop playing the game then," he said.

Caty pursed her lips. "No, let's keep doing it. I wanna see how far you'll go 'til you take a dare."

Elan laughed. "Not happening."

"Oh, don't dare me."

He shrugged.

"Stop shrugging." She laid a hand on his shoulder. "It's unattractive."

"Shrugging is unattractive?"

"Not your turn," she pointed out. "I'm gonna think about my next question for a while."

"What about me?"

"You think about it too." She took a bite of her chicken. "Make it interesting. Not about our daily lives."

"So, existential?"

"Yeah, if that's your thing."

She started eating, so Elan did too. They were quiet as they ate. He thought about his question but was more worried about hers.

When they were done, they paid for their meals and walked back to the hotel. She kept giving him looks, as if gauging what he had come up with. The truth was he had nothing.

The elevator opened, and they got in, standing face to face, each in a corner.

"You ready?" she asked after the doors opened on their floor.

He stepped out of the elevator and followed. Caty stopped in front of the room, reached for the key card, and turned around, her back blocking the door. "Should I ask you now?"

Elan felt nervous. In the amount of time it took her to think of one question, he'd imagined a dozen stupid things she might ask. He nodded. "Yeah."

Caty took a deep breath. "Would you like to come in?"

He thought she'd ask something more personal or poke fun at the state of his nose.

"That's it? That was the question you've been holding out on me the whole time?"

"Can't a girl eat in silence?"

He suppressed a smile. Elan dropped his hand, rocked back on his heels, and shoved his hands in his pockets. "I mean, sure."

"And no, that wasn't the question. I'm just easing you into it." She kept her hands on the door handle.

He licked his lips.

She finally took a step closer, raised a hand to his collar, and straightened the edge of it before she looked him in the eyes. "Elan. Kiss me."

Elan swallowed. Caty let go of his collar and brushed her hands over his shirt. She leaned in close enough for him to feel her breath on his face. If he just inched closer . . .

"That's not a question," he pointed out.

She held her breath, he noticed, as her hand rested on his chest. She managed a smile. "Then how come you're making me ask for it again?"

Please?

She wanted to say it out loud, but wouldn't that sound a little desperate? She didn't want to admit it, but in a way, she was desperate for company. That had been true for a while now. She was looking for companionship when she went to

Otto's, but instead she got chased by his much younger girlfriend. *Fiancée.* She really needed to get used to that. Obviously, Otto was never gonna leave Madeline, not when he let her chase away other girls.

I'm in my mid-twenties, I'm not having a midlife crisis, she reminded herself. *I'm young. I'm still young.*

She lingered, her body a mere inch away from his, the warmth already spreading on her skin.

"Yes."

She was about to go to another place, obsessing about her looks and her age when Elan spoke. It made her jump. He grabbed her shoulders and backed her into the wooden door, her head hitting it with a dull thud.

"Oh, shit." He fumbled, palming the back of her head and feeling for bumps.

"Ow." She grimaced, putting a hand on her neck as well.

He seemed to understand that she really was hurt. "Sorry, I—"

"Was trying to knock me out?" Caty felt Elan's fingers thread around her hair, feeling her head.

She closed her eyes, whimpering a little, and Elan inched closer. He started to rub her scalp, massaging her head softly.

"Is this even helping?"

Caty opened her eyes and met his, and she thought she saw something happen, like a click, a spark of life reignited.

She simply licked her lips and nodded.

"Sorry, I wasn't trying to hurt you," Elan said, his voice soft and low.

His fingers were still massaging her scalp, and she exhaled in relief. He was good at this—who knew? He had magical fingers.

Caty closed her eyes again, a small smile forming on her lips. Her shoulders loosened, responding to his touch. The back of her head no longer hurt much, and close to him, her body softened.

Elan's fingers slid back down on her neck, then paused. "You okay now?"

Slowly, as if assessing herself, she nodded.

"I was trying to do it your way."

She frowned. "My way?"

"You know, when you first kissed me, you kind of just grabbed me."

"Yeah, but I pulled you in. You pushed me back." She laughed.

He scratched his temple while his other hand rested on her neck. "I miscalculated."

"Sure you're not getting back at me for annoying you so much?"

He pulled his other hand away. "Would I even do this if I'm still annoyed at you?"

"Remorse is another thing."

It looked as if he was about to tell her something serious, but he hesitated. He was shutting her out again, and she'd worked so hard to get him to open up.

She took his hand. "Tell me the truth, Elan."

She felt as if she was groping in the dark to keep him like this. Close to her, open, willing.

"I think it's my turn to ask you a question, actually."

Oh, that's right. The game. She'd almost forgotten about it. She already had him close to her, and that was the point of it, really. To make him feel comfortable around her. "You didn't answer my question properly."

"Are you sure it doesn't hurt anymore?"

She nodded, but her hand held on to his, asking him to let it stay there. She had missed the sensation of having someone hold and caress her.

"Shame," Elan inhaled. "Would've kissed it to make it better."

She couldn't help but smile. That was unexpected. Hoped for, but yes, unexpected. Really, she shouldn't have underestimated Elan's game so much. After all, she was trapped between a door and a man. She did want him, even when he was being a Judy. Maybe he's got this all in the bag.

She pressed her lips together to stop herself from smiling so much.

Elan smiled back. She felt his thumb run along her nape again, which made her moan quietly. Caty bowed her head, partly embarrassed at the sound she'd made. But she felt him dip his head, his nose against the skin of her neck until, finally, his lips touched it. It was warm, fleeting at first, but he followed up quickly. He began planting soft kisses on her neck, not even where it hurt, but did it matter?

She reached up to the back of his head, caressing it as his kisses reached her jaw, her cheek. She gasped when he lowered his mouth to her neck, sucked on it for a second, before his lips parted.

Caty was still, waiting for the next step—a kiss, a graze, a freaking breath—*Why, why did it stop?*

He pulled away, straightened his back, and looked her in the eyes. She stared at him, her face probably asking the question she had been screaming inside: *Why?*

Just then the door of the next room opened, and a middle-aged man stepped out, quite surprised to see them in the hallway.

"Good afternoon," Elan mumbled, reaching out for Caty's hand and grabbing the key card.

Caty let him open the door, and they jumped quickly into the room to make the whole thing less humiliating.

She laughed as he closed the door. "Did he see?"

Elan tilted his head, grimacing, "Yeah, probably."

Caty walked over to the bed and sat on the edge. She took off her shoes, aware that he was still standing right by the door, watching her. She saw the confusion and frustration in his face when their eyes met. The frustration she could help with, but the confusion?

"Do you want to go?" she asked, taking a gamble. There was a big chance he would say yes and bolt out of the place so fast she wouldn't be able to find him ever again. She could still feel the sensation of his lips on her neck, the sliver of his tongue on her skin. Strangely, it made her feel brave enough to ask, as if that was protection against him saying no.

Elan put his hands on his hips, licked his lips, and looked up at the ceiling, as if the answers were all there.

She slid up the bed, lifted up the covers, and left the space next to her.

He looked at her, and his eyes told a different story now: less confusion, more like hunger, wanting—completely different from the looks he had given her all day.

Elan walked—no, sprinted—to the bed and pulled her up by her shoulders so she was on her knees. He stood right by the bed, holding her tightly as he looked her right in the eyes.

"Just stay, okay?" she asked, slowly reaching out to him.

He breathed out, and it released some of his tension. Quietly, he nodded.

She was the first to kiss him again.

Their first kiss hadn't been like this. She'd been in control that time: she'd known what she had to do to keep him hooked. She'd known when to stop, to keep him wanting more. She stopped the kiss early to set the bait, leaving a zing of electricity lingering on her lips when she pulled away.

She knew he had felt it too. He had looked at her differently since that first kiss, as if she had something he needed. It was a complete one-eighty from how the day had started, when she had felt like the loser.

Caty might have kissed Elan first, but this time felt more like a collision. Her senses were deafened by the sound of her heartbeat, her whole body softened to every movement, and no one was pulling back. It seemed like a battle—who wanted more, who needed more, who could give more.

She needed this. She needed him. Not just to get her out of the house or to get her out of the situation with Otto. Now she needed him to help shake off the bad feelings she'd been trying to get rid of. He was doing a pretty good job of it so far, taking her mind off other things and making her notice that his hands had begun to roam.

It's funny to think they were practically strangers, because everything was beginning to feel familiar. She was starting to crave the sensation of his arms around her waist and the feel of his mouth pressed against her skin.

There was a moment of hesitation, but Caty put her hands over his to lead Elan—to allow him to explore new territories, uncover skin.

His fingers skimmed right under her shirt, and it was like lighting a match to her insides. His kisses poured gasoline, fed the flame.

They broke apart, and their lips moved for only a breath. She pushed forward, but he held her back as he leaned his forehead toward hers. His voice was a ragged whisper, "Are we . . . ?"

She smiled, felt her cheeks burn as she licked her already swollen lips. "Yes."

four

He could tell he was falling apart. Everything that had been calm and calculated earlier—careful, he'd like to think—had gotten clumsy, messy, and frantic very fast.

It was the way she looked when she said *yes.* Her cheeks were flushed, her lips were pink and plump, and he'd done that to her. He couldn't tell if he felt awe or relief when she said it, pulled the shirt off his back, and began kissing his neck.

She pulled him in, and they stumbled to the bed. They did not land on it gracefully, but that was okay because they were preoccupied with discarding each other's clothing as fast as they could. He managed to take off her shirt, and she unbuttoned his pants.

They stared at each other for a while, taking in the sight: both half-naked and very much still into the moment. Caty lay on her back, and he followed suit, positioning himself on top, careful not to put his weight on her.

He paused, his nose touching hers before kissing her again.

She moaned, enveloping him in her arms, pulling him closer. Her legs wrapped around his hips, and it was so tempting to just sink into it, to just lose himself and let go.

"You have protection, right?" Caty asked, in between the kisses.

If he were honest, he'd tell her that he'd love to just kiss her more. They were so good at it, and he wanted to better know her sighs, the side of her jaw, the hollow of her neck, her clavicle, and the rest of her he hadn't seen, or touched, or kissed.

But her hand was already on his stomach, crawling down to reach out for him.

Elan paused, lifted his body up just an inch. "What's the hurry?"

Her hand stilled. "I'm dying, that's all."

Elan lurched away from her momentarily to locate his pants on the floor. He heard Caty laugh—no, giggle.

He looked back. "What?"

She let her head fall back on the pillow, still laughing. He found his wallet with the condom hidden inside, but now he wasn't sure if it was still needed.

Elan stood over the bed and asked, "What?"

"Nothing," she answered, laughter subsiding. "You did nothing wrong, just get back here."

He fished out the condom from his wallet, frowning.

She sat up. "Aw, are you upset?"

"I don't know about you, but I don't think laughing is actually encouraging."

"What kind of sex have you been having?" Caty asked, looking at the pack he was holding.

Elan thought about the question, but he couldn't exactly remember. And why would he when he's got a beautiful girl sitting in front of him, biting her lip?

"Hey," Caty called for his attention, "do you need me to do anything for you?"

There were plenty of things she could do for him, but he also knew there were plenty of things he would like to do for her too.

She leaned in and carefully placed a hand on his shoulder, as if she was learning to do this again, to get close to him. She was so unbelievably coy that he had the urge to grab her ass and pull her in.

He felt her gasp, lips right by his jaw. "Judy," she sang, teasing. "Why did you laugh?"

"No reason." Caty kissed his earlobe, and it tickled him. He didn't respond, so she leaned back. "*Fine*. I was laughing because I thought, *Juliana must be an idiot*."

Elan blinked.

"And also because I was checking you out when you bent down, that's all. Cute butt."

But he barely heard that. The first thing she said had struck him more deeply. *Juliana must be an idiot*. What did she mean with that?

"Okay?" Caty squeezed his arm.

He looked at the condom still in his hands then back at her. Her eyes looked up at him expectantly, but he was lost in his head.

"Elan," she called, but instead he turned away. His thoughts were spinning. He felt her hand on his arm and then on his face. She slapped his jaw lightly, turning his face to look him in the eyes. "You okay?"

"No, I . . ." *What was his problem?* Elan looked around, painfully aware that the room was too cold and they were almost naked. They were doing it, or were about to, if he could just snap out of whatever was happening to him.

Her hand reached out for him again, but he moved away. *What the hell*.

"Okay," Caty said, moving back.

This is Juliana's friend. He knew that. Was he thinking about that when he was kissing her? Not really. When she unbuttoned his pants? Not at all. He had to think about that now? She had to bring up Juliana?

Elan looked at her and felt his insides stir. Earlier, she'd been so bold, as if it was the most common event. She didn't even want to dim the lights or cover herself up. She was just being her, with him, and he couldn't deny that he wanted to stare at her a little longer.

But now she just looked embarrassed. She pulled the sheets over her body and stared at him questioningly.

"I'm sorry," Elan looked away, the disappointment hitting him fast. "I can't."

He can't? Did that just slip out of his mouth? Caty was completely still, her hand clutching the sheets. Could he blame her? He was stunned to have uttered those words. At least part of him had been yelling, *Just fucking do it.* Caty was beautiful, with her tangled hair, flushed cheeks, and absolutely distracting lips. Jesus Christ, he can't do it? Really?

She inhaled, then let go of the breath, silently. Calmly. Finally, she said, "It's okay. You're right. We can't do it. Who are we kidding?"

We can't? he thought, still sitting on the bed. He watched her get up and pick up her clothes from the floor.

"So, you're in love with her," she announced, like it was now a known fact. "You're not good at denying it."

"I wasn't . . ." he mumbled but didn't finish. He felt pathetic, not knowing what to say to her. Was she right? Was he in love with Jules? Was that why he couldn't do this?

"I have this problem. I always do," she continued.

His eyes followed her as she walked around putting her clothes back on.

"What?"

"I tend to like the guys who like Juliana." She paused. "But I'm also attracted to unavailable men. At least that's what my therapist said."

"You have a therapist?" His voice was an octave too high.

"No," Caty sighed. "Well, I had one when I had an accident way back. My friend isn't really my therapist, but he studied psychology to please his parents because they wanted him to be a doctor."

She tucked her hair behind her ear. "I'm babbling."

Elan gulped.

Caty resumed putting her clothes back on. "I'm attracted to you for all the wrong reasons. I could hear him telling me that."

It was a nail in his coffin. Elan glumly stared down at himself, now the only one naked and freezing in the room. *This is your fault. You said you can't,* he thought.

"Now that that's established," she inhaled, getting all serious, "don't feel bad about it. I kissed you first. We were in the moment. I was seeking validation. My therapist would also say that."

Caty tilted her head at him. "You seem as if you needed . . . something too. We were doing each other a service."

"A service," he repeated. But he hadn't given her what she needed.

"And you don't even like me."

"Not true," he was quick to refute.

"Yeah? What do you like about me?"

He wanted to raise his hand and gesture at all of her, but he didn't. It just seemed as if *that* wasn't her point.

"You seem interesting," he managed.

Caty laughed. She stepped closer and ruffled his hair, as if he was a kid. "Oh, honey. You have no idea."

Two for two. How low can one go after today, really? First, she was ditched by Otto. Then Madeline chased her. Second, she was rejected by this guy who she thought was honestly into her. Well, maybe she was more into him, but Elan liked her enough, she reckoned, and that was fine. She wasn't going to marry him—she just wanted some attention. She was longing for that feeling of being wanted again. And she'd felt it with him; she was sure. He was with her when they were sucking each other's faces, wasn't he?

What the hell happened?

She headed to the bathroom, and before closing the door, she told him, "Just go."

She turned on the shower, and the sound filled the bathroom, comforting her a bit. She leaned back on the door and tried to hear what was going on in the room.

He could go; he *should* go.

How many hours did she have left before she flew out of the country? This was exactly why she didn't stay in the Philippines for too long. She just had the worst luck here.

She closed her eyes and prayed *please, please, please,* until she heard movement. Feet shuffling. He's probably getting dressed.

Caty turned back, faced the door, and waited.

A couple of minutes passed then nothing. Her hand hovered over the knob until she heard the door open and close.

So he did go.

She dropped her hand. She should have just stayed alone this whole day. Why the hell did she think that having some company would be a good idea? Especially when she barely knew him?

She stared at herself in the mirror. Her eyes looked tired, her hair was a mess, and her eye makeup needed a touch-up. Instead of repairing the damage, she took the rest of her clothes off and stepped into the shower. It was freezing cold, and she shuddered as soon as the water hit her head and shoulders, but she let it soak her.

If she could drown the memory of this day, she would.

When she was done, she took her time with the hair dryer and what little makeup she had in her purse. She managed to smile at her reflection.

She'd be okay. She just needed to get back to Toronto.

She had some time to nap before her alarm went off; then she called reception. No one was answering, though, so she went down to ask for a cab.

As soon as the elevator doors opened, she saw him waiting for her in the lobby.

She quickly pushed the elevator button to close the doors again before he could get up from his seat. She gulped.

Great, what's the plan? Hide in the elevator? She had to go out; she knew that. She just had to walk out of the elevator then straight to the door with her head up. She could get her own cab.

Caty took a deep breath and pressed the open button.

He was still there. *What the hell is he still doing here?* He looked confused at what she did. If she had cared, she would have explained. But she had a plan: walk out, head up.

She focused on the glass doors. He didn't follow her, thank God, and she managed to get out fine.

It was still pitch dark, and the guard jolted from his sleep when he saw her.

"Taxi, ma'am?" he asked.

Caty nodded. The guard rubbed his eyes and stumbled out into the street to hail a cab.

"I'll take you," she heard.

Caty ignored him. In her periphery, she saw him walk up to her until he was just a foot away.

"We don't have to talk," he offered.

Caty paused. She watched the guard struggle to get a cab, as the streets were void of vehicles.

She just needed to get out of this country. *Fast.* But if that meant spending a couple of humiliating moments with this guy again . . .

Well, it's not like the worst hadn't already happened.

"You don't have to sit next to me."

She turned, deciding that her desire to leave the country was stronger than her desire to avoid him. So she handed him her bag as if he was her chauffeur and said, "Let's go."

The drive back was very quiet. Sure, Elan had wanted quiet earlier, but not now. It was awkward and uncomfortable and just . . . *wrong.* He'd waited in the hotel lobby for hours because he couldn't just go, but he couldn't stay with her either.

They arrived at the airport, and she quickly thanked him and started to open the door.

Elan hurried around the car to catch the door and held it open for her.

"You don't have to do that," she said.

"Look, I'm . . ."

Caty shook her head. "Don't. You're gonna make it worse."

He'd been about to apologize, but would that make it worse? She deserved the apology—he was the one who'd messed up.

"Look, let's just drop it," Caty continued. "I mean, who knows? We might actually have a shot at being friends. We already got rid of the sexual stuff."

Elan wasn't expecting that. How would leaving each other sexually frustrated give them a shot at being friends? Maybe it was one of those things, an ice cream cone: something nice and sweet

---

to tell someone before it melts. This girl lived in another country, and he had a full life here. Not to mention the fact that he may have been in love with another girl for the last two years. Sex or not, he and Caty were not made to last longer than this day.

But he decided to hand her an ice cream cone too. "Good, I could use one of those."

Caty smirked. "Especially now that you're gonna break up with Juliana, right?"

He frowned. "Why would I break up with her?"

"This is a fact," she said, holding up a finger. "Once a girl gets a boyfriend, she loses her two closest friends. Those girls she was roomies with in college? They're as good as barnacles on her ship."

She continued, "Juliana and I just made up. I'm her boyfriend's sister, so it's not gonna be me, Judy."

"So you assume she's gonna drop me?"

"There are too many people in her life," Caty argued. "She has fantastic parents too. How can a person be that loved?"

Elan pursed his lips and shrugged.

"You heard me, right?" She raised an eyebrow. "She has a boyfriend. *You are not him.*"

He bowed his head, then nodded.

She must have felt bad for him because she laid her hand on his shoulder. He was getting used to that—it was her habit. "It's okay. You'll find someone else."

Was she actually comforting him? After what he did to her?

He looked at her and thought, *I really liked this girl.* Regret hit him right then and there, and he felt the pain sink in.

"I hope you don't take this the wrong way," Caty started, "but I hope I never see you again."

Elan met her eyes, mouth agape. *How do I respond to that?*

She smiled and said, "It's for your sanity."

He didn't get it, but he simply nodded. He'd missed it. He had mighty fucking missed this one.

"But if I see you elsewhere, I'll say hi." Caty lifted her hand to pinch his chin. "Promise me you'll be happy to see me too?"

He sighed, nodding his head slowly.

"So much for living up to your name, Elan."

"I'll change it to something else," he retorted.

"Judy?"

He laughed, his hand finally touching hers. He felt the electricity that shot up between them. He mentally kicked himself in the ass for being such a disappointment.

"I didn't do a web check-in, so I'll . . ." She jerked her hand away and pointed toward the entrance.

"Right."

"All right." Caty took a deep breath. "Guess this is it."

Elan lifted his arm to wave. "Have a good flight."

She was lingering, and so was he. They had been saying goodbye to each other for half a day, and it still felt too soon to say it. Caty took a tiny step toward him.

"For what it's worth, you were great at making out."

He tried to repress a smile.

"Gee, thanks, Caty," she mimicked him. "You were great too."

Elan felt a tug inside his chest, and he smiled. The way she was looking at him now was making it even harder for him to say anything.

So he said nothing and dipped his head down to kiss her instead. He wasn't too polite about it either, cupping her face with his hands and taking her lips fully.

Why had they stopped kissing in the first place? *His fault. Right.* He started to pull away, but he felt her fingers run up his chest, grabbing him by the collar of his shirt and reeling him back in.

They broke away grinning, his forehead brushing hers.

"Now, that's how you do it *my way*." Her hand rested on his nape, and she kissed his neck softly, a heated graze that made him feel warm inside.

His back hit the side mirror of the car and it hurt, but he didn't care. Nothing could distract him now.

"Sorry," he groaned. "I can't let you leave thinking that I didn't—"

Caty patted his chest as she pulled away. "Checking in."

"You don't have any luggage."

"Right." She tiptoed and met his mouth again, tongues sliding back and hands roaming the skin underneath clothes. "God, I'm supposed to hate you."

"Oh, got you covered. Been hating myself too."

Caty kissed him one more time, two, maybe three, before completely stepping back on her heels. She cleared her throat. "Okay, that's . . . see? I'm good at that too. We made quite a show for those nosy old ladies."

She pointed to their direction and waved them off. He felt his cheeks warm.

"Don't say anything more." Caty took another step back. "Let's leave it at that, okay?"

He knew what she meant. They should leave it while it was still good, before they ruined it. So he agreed. He took another look at her, as if to take a mental picture. Despite the dark rim under her eyes from staying up that night and her creased clothes, she looked quite resplendent.

Elan shrugged, with a smile to match hers.

"Classic Elan," Caty teased, as if they knew enough about each other to have inside jokes. She finally turned after a quick wave.

As he leaned back on his car, his smile spread into a silly grin, and all Elan could do was watch her leave.

PART

Two

We can all begin freely—a slight preference is natural enough;
but there are very few of us who have heart enough to be
really in love without encouragement.

JANE AUSTEN

five

NINE MONTHS LATER

It could be worse. For one thing, she could be wearing the wrong dress, but she wasn't. She looked gorgeous in this dress. And why shouldn't she? Caty had lined up for a warehouse sale to get it. She'd elbowed women out of the way to have it.

When her roommate Lucian asked her why she'd bought such a ridiculously embellished gold gown, she told him she was saving it for a special occasion. She tried it on and showed him, and he said she looked like a trophy.

Good, Caty thought. She wanted to look like a trophy. She wanted to look like gold. She wanted to be first prize. Not second, not third; she wanted to be first.

So she carried the gold gown home, kept it in the bag, stored it carefully, and didn't wear it again until this night.

When she walked out of her room and met her brother, Kip, he gave her a look and said, "You know this isn't your party, right?"

Caty smirked. "Shut up, Crispin."

He shuddered hearing his real name. "I mean, you look great."

She did. The gown's top was embellished with gold appliques and sequins, held together by thin spaghetti straps. The dress cascaded into pure tulle and flowed as she moved, exposing a good portion of her leg every time she put her right foot forward. The back was scooped way down, almost to her waist.

She kept her hair down in a messy wave, and it fell below her shoulders, framing her face well. She'd grown out her bangs and dyed her hair red. It worked well with her skin tone, brown-red lips, and, of course, the gold gown.

"I know," she just answered. "But you should really save your compliments for your girlfriend."

Caty walked ahead of him, knowing he was only waiting outside the room for Juliana, who just stepped out. She was wearing a red sheath dress with a halter neckline and a slit just a couple of inches above her knee—simpler and more modest than what Caty wore, but she looked so good in red that even Caty whistled when she came into view.

It was the Coronados' thirtieth wedding anniversary, and Juliana's parents had decided to renew their vows that afternoon. This evening, the family was having dinner and drinks with the rest of the town—including the mayor and his wife, the bored trophy wives of the Tourism Club, and their sons and daughters. There was a club for events like this, and the party was called a "ball." For such a small town, people did like to make something big out of things like thirty years of marriage, a new fountain on the plaza, the fiesta, or someone's eighteenth birthday.

Caty was here with her mother for the occasion and also to get her fix of sunshine. It was pretty cold in Toronto, and like a bird, she needed to leave to survive.

Since they got the invitation for the wedding anniversary two months ago, her brother, Kip, had been pestering them to attend. He'd decided to stay in the Philippines so he could take over the company their father started with Juliana's dad—and be in the same country as his girlfriend. Caty knew she had to show up. For moral support, she figured.

It had only been nine months since Caty was last in San Juan. She thought about her last day and quickly winced, glancing at her brother and Juliana's public display of affection instead. Seeing him kiss Juliana's wrist as she reached out to caress his face was way better than recalling how humiliating that last day in the Philippines had been.

She really was hoping she'd have better luck this time.

She wondered how it could work here, dating in a small town. Caty was certain everyone had been talking about Juliana and Kip since they first started showing up in places together. She shuddered as she imagined how people would have speculated. It was the town's hobby. Some people liked to call it "caring for the community," but she'd never been a fan of it. Especially when she'd been a target not so long ago.

That's why she could never live here again. She couldn't deal with people nosing around.

Caty cleared her throat, and Juliana turned to her. "I can go first, if you guys need more time?"

Juliana answered, "No, we're good. Let's go."

Kip and Juliana's hands interlaced as if it was automatic, and they walked toward her.

"Great." Caty smiled, turning around before she sighed. They started down the stairs to the party.

Caty hoped she'd have more time to enjoy the night, but looking around the whole room, she already knew it would be hard.

Good thing she had her gold dress on. She had seen it in a magazine and knew she had to have it. Some girls might picture their wedding dresses, but Caty pictured the dress she'd wear when she finally got her revenge.

That's what the gold dress was for.

That's what tonight was about.

That's why she thought it wouldn't be so bad to come home again after all.

Had he been transformed or what? Elan had driven the roads to San Juan so many times in the last nine months that he could probably close his eyes and get there—not that he ever would.

The first time, he had to get his car. The second time, he had to take something back to Juliana. At first, Kip wasn't happy that he kept coming back, but they got to talking and began this weird friendship. He kept coming back because despite being a city boy, he had discovered the town's charm. The little quirks, the easiness of the lifestyle, the fresh air.

Of course, there was that girl he was waiting to see. He knew Caty wouldn't come back just yet, but he kept hearing her name in conversations. Sometimes she was mentioned several times, sometimes never at all. Whenever he heard it, he tried not to appear too interested. He'd look down, rub a hand across his jaw, and ask polite follow-up questions.

What he found out about her during these fleeting conversations was that she used to be in love with another man, she liked to dance, she had a car accident with Juliana when they were sixteen that eventually made her move to Toronto, and, finally, the most important information: she was coming home for the Coronados' wedding anniversary.

So Elan hauled himself back to San Juan. This time, he wouldn't just hear her name in conversations. She would be there.

The ball was his first San Juan party. Juliana told him to wear a suit, which he thought was strange in such an easygoing place. But Kip explained that was how people partied in San Juan. Good thing his boss, Pascual, knew where he could rent a suit and sent him there in time for the trip.

He rented a black suit that fit him perfectly. That's one less thing to worry about, he thought, and now he only needed to worry about what he would say when he met Caty again.

Elan wanted to come up with something clever, but she was the clever one, and he only fed off what she handed him. Days after their time together, Elan realized he was still thinking about Caty simply because he had never met anyone like her.

She was different and intriguing, and he beat himself up for the impression he must have made on her. His sensible self tried to compensate, convinced that if they had gone too far that night, then what? Where would they go from there?

He had to convince himself that choosing not to have sex that night actually gave him a chance to be more than just a one-time thing.

The Coronados' party was at Casa Isabella, and he checked himself into one of the hotel's eleven rooms. It was a small hotel, because no one ever went to San Juan. If one did, there was usually a family or a friend who offered a place to stay.

Elan had once crashed in Kip's apartment, but he quickly realized he got in the way of Jules coming over for the night, so he never did it again. He had been a loyal patron of Casa Isabella, with its old-time Spanish Colonial-era styled rooms, floor-to-ceiling curtains, and ghost stories from the cleaning ladies. He hadn't seen any ghosts, but it did get eerily quiet.

"Mr. Aguirre, back again for the ball, I assume?" Celia, the receptionist, great-granddaughter of *the* Isabella of the Casa, welcomed him as soon as he arrived.

He smiled. "Yes. Am I the only one staying here tonight?"

"We're fully booked; good thing you made your reservations early."

The ball was just about to start, and he only needed a few minutes to change into his suit, splash some water on his face, and talk himself into doing what he had been planning.

Tonight, he wasn't just going to attend this party.

He was going to talk to Caty, make sure she remembered him, find a way to somehow redeem himself for making her feel unwanted that night, and end this night without any regrets.

That was a tall order, but it was the plan. He had been making it since the day she flew out.

It would have been easier if she'd just left Otto. Why hadn't she? Caty shook her head. *Don't ask that question.* She sighed and glared at the woman wearing a green dress. She really should hate Madeline, but the girl knew how to pick a dress. She also knew how to style herself. Her hair was in a neat bun to accentuate her long neck, and she looked effortless—Grace Kelly–esque, classic, and divine.

There was no point in hating Madeline. Caty was just like her.

Hating Otto? Well, that was different. She glanced again at the couple and cursed. That man could wear a suit. He'd always had a wonderful gait. Despite the rumors that he'd been sick over Christmas, Otto still looked better than anyone else at the party. He radiated confidence, and he knew how to give it and take it away from anyone around him.

"Don't stare," Caty heard her brother say. He was sitting next to her watching the parade of people coming in.

She laughed and insisted, "I wasn't. I was just looking."

Juliana was tending to her parents as part of her maid of honor duties and had left them both sitting at their table.

"Whatever happened to that guy you were dating in Toronto?" Kip asked.

A wrinkle formed on her forehead. "Who, Sean? I don't know. I guess we stopped dating."

"Why? I liked him."

"Then you date him." She stuck out her tongue at him.

Kip sighed. "You can do so much better than Otto."

"Why, 'cause he's way older than me?"

"No." Kip ran a hand over his mouth. "One, he's married. And now that you've mentioned that, yeah. We've known him since we were kids. It's creepy."

"He was just friends with Dad; he's not the same age!" He was fifteen years older than her. She wasn't dating her grandpa.

Kip shook his head but didn't say anything more.

Caty rolled her eyes and explained, "Whatever. He is married, and I wasn't even staring. I was just checking. I didn't think he'd be here; they said he was sick or something?"

Kip nodded. "We didn't know how serious it was. Madeline was trying to be mum about it. But yeah, he hadn't been at any town events for a while."

She pursed her lips, annoyed that for once, the town's chitchat didn't help her out. She wanted to know more. Should she be worried about him? But that wasn't her job anymore—was it ever?

"Anyway, I want to see you happy."

"I am happy," Caty snapped.

Kip glanced at her, and she rewarded him with a sheepish smile. His look told her that he doubted it, so she had to steer it back to him.

"Are you happy, here?" she asked.

His eyes went back to the room, and his face beamed, "Yes."

She followed the direction of his gaze and found Juliana talking to some people as she made her way back to her parents' table. Caty snickered and shook her head, "I've never seen you this dopey. It's disgusting."

"But it doesn't feel like that at all."

Caty cringed. "Oh God, you're gonna talk about it. I saw you kiss a girl once, and I was really traumatized. I'm gonna go through that again if you start talking like this."

"Whom did you see me with?"

"I forgot her name. You were thirteen. I wanted to scratch my eyes out."

Kip grinned. "Ah, Lauren. Great. You saw my first kiss."

"It wasn't great. I hope you've improved. Otherwise, it's my obligation as Juliana's best friend to tell her to get a better boyfriend."

Kip laughed but let it slide. He cleared his throat and asked, "Is Mom okay?"

"Yeah." She looked around to check where their mother was. She had been mingling with guests, sitting with her friends instead of her kids. "Why?"

Kip pointed over at their mother, talking to a man.

"Oh," Caty's smile widened. Since their father's death, their mother hadn't entertained a lot of suitors, and they were always on the lookout to see how she was doing. Not that they were looking for a new dad—God, no—they just wanted to make sure their mother wasn't hesitating to start something new because of them. "That's new."

He nodded, taking a drink of water. "Do you even know who he is?"

"Why are you asking me? You live here. Maybe they're just talking."

"Yeah. I'm gonna stop watching now." He pushed his chair back, "Are you gonna be okay here?"

"Yeah." She nodded. "Please. I'm not four. Go."

Kip leaned in to kiss her cheek and advised, "Stop staring too."

She snorted, "I honestly didn't see them 'til you pointed them out."

"Not Mom. I meant the other couple. Your dress looks better when it's walking around, mingling, having fun, and not stalking other people."

She shooed him. "Go away."

"I'm serious. I want you happy."

She watched him walk away and approach Juliana. Her eyes darted back to Otto and Madeline's table, and she felt her face fall.

How did she picture this night again? She'd wanted to enter the room, focus on Otto, and see that look on his face, the one he used to give her all the time, as if she was the most delightful thing in the room.

Today he hadn't even spared her a glance. It was like she wasn't even there. And she knew she was hard to ignore. She'd made it a point to be seen; she even looked like a goddamned trophy!

Yet in every way, she still felt like a loser.

six

"You made it."

Elan turned and found Kip, one of the two people he knew in San Juan. Elan was hanging out next to the speakers, basically hiding until he found his friends. Or until they found him.

"I told you I'd come."

"Aren't you deaf by now? That can't be good for your eardrums."

Elan laughed and took a couple of steps away from the speakers. "Where's Jules?"

"Maid of honor duties." He turned and pointed. Elan focused on the girl in the red dress and nodded.

"Did the Coronados see you yet?" Kip asked.

"Yes, after I checked in."

They remained like that for a second, two men standing side by side, watching the crowd. Kip drew in a breath. "So my sister's at that table."

"Is she?"

Kip smirked. "Hell, I saw you looking over at our table a couple of times. You are not subtle at all."

"She didn't seem to notice."

"Well that's because she's . . . preoccupied at the moment."

"Is she okay?"

Kip sighed. "She will be. She always picks herself up when she's down."

That made Elan smile.

"Sometimes she needs a little boost, though." He threw Elan a glance.

Elan took a step forward and asked, "Is this all right with you?"

"Why are you asking me? She's the one you should be asking first. Then you can check with me."

Elan grinned. It made sense. He hadn't been sure about Kip when they first met, but the guy really grew on him. Elan considered him a good friend, sensible, and at times wiser than he was himself. It was in Kip's nature to push people to do their best.

"All right, then I'll go ahead and find out the answer." Elan turned around and headed for Caty's table.

He was hoping for a more natural approach, but he realized that he should do just the opposite this time. He'd met Caty by accident the first time, so he should meet her tonight simply because he sought her out. He wanted to do it that way, and he was going to stick to the plan.

Before Elan could approach the table, Caty's eyes wandered, and she noticed him. For a second, she didn't seem to recognize him, but he saw her eyes widen in recognition before she pursed her lips.

It was exactly how he pictured she'd react.

She kept her mouth pursed, as if deciding whether or not to acknowledge him. The former won, and her face broke into a smile. Relief washed over him.

He walked over and sat in the chair next to hers.

"What, are you still here?" she retorted.

He paused, then said, "The party's barely started."

"Still following Juliana around?"

Ah, that argument. Elan smiled at how they were picking up where they left off. As if no days passed in between and they were still continuing the conversation they'd been having.

"I am not following her around. I'm being her friend."

Caty straightened her back. She looked off into the distance, and he tried to follow her gaze but couldn't be sure what she was looking at. So he said, "You look great."

"I've heard that one before. What else you got for me?" she answered, looking back at him for only a second.

"I see you haven't changed."

Caty turned to him, chin dropping coyly to her shoulder as she pouted. "They say you shouldn't fix what's not broken."

"I wasn't complaining."

Elan turned around and squinted to see what she'd been staring at. She couldn't seem to stop watching whatever it was that had caught her attention a few seconds ago.

As he scanned the crowd, he thought, *Boy, the whole place is filled with people I don't know.* In spite of his recent visits to the town, Elan still felt like a guest. He was an outsider. He now understood that these people knew each other very well. Everyone had a relative here.

"How are you?"

"Doing all right, I guess." His shoulders lifted into a shrug. He stopped midway, but what else could he do? It was already a shrug.

"I see *you* haven't changed." Caty glanced at him, letting her gaze drop to his feet and slide back up to his face. "But you don't look so bad yourself, Judy."

"Thanks." For a moment, he thought he'd found someone oddly familiar in the crowd. He tried to remember where he'd seen her but couldn't place her properly.

"Got any plans for the night?"

"Not really," he answered and did it again. He shrugged. Elan bowed his head and peeked at her to see her reaction.

She was smiling but still not fully looking at him. He couldn't tell if that smile was for him or somebody else. He felt slightly annoyed, but more at himself. He took a deep breath and waited, counting before leaning his arm on the table and drawing closer to her. He blocked her view and caught her eye.

Caty's eyes widened, and Elan felt her gaze swipe across his lips before looking him squarely in the eyes.

"Hi," he greeted.

Her face softened as she offered him a smile. "You wanna do something else tonight?"

"Like what?"

"I don't know. Something fun. I'm already bored."

"Like sneak out?"

Caty's eyes narrowed. "I like where you're going with this. Then do what?"

"I don't know."

"We can drive by the beach. You have a car, right?"

"Yeah."

"Do you think we can steal some liquor here?"

Elan's snorted. "Or we can buy it, you know. We're allowed to do that now."

Caty sighed and leaned back in her chair. "Oh, that's right. I almost forgot. You're not the fun one."

He opened his mouth to protest, but obviously she was not done.

"I guess I've forgotten most of what happened that night," she said, looking away. "Seeing that it was horrible."

Elan laughed. "It wasn't that bad."

Caty winced. "Are you serious? Are you listening to yourself? No man could think that was good."

He knew exactly what she meant. Of course it wasn't good. That was his fault. "I didn't say it was."

"But you said it wasn't that bad."

Elan tilted his head, the edge of his lips curling. "Fine. Let me redeem myself then."

She gave him a patronizing smile, but then realization settled on her face. Caty cleared her throat and reached out to his tie, her fingers fumbling at it. "Do you mean it?"

He blinked and felt the tug of her hand. He'd thought about this moment. He'd pictured it in his head several times a day since they met. There were different scenarios. In his head, she still looked the same: radiant skin and jet-black, shoulder-length hair with bangs resting on her forehead . . .

But he hadn't pictured her as she was now. It was as if she'd leaped out of Botticelli's *The Birth of Venus,* for fuck's sake, with her nude-gold dress and red hair. Her lips were not the shade of scarlet he remembered; the color was something deeper and earthy, like terra-cotta. It made him wonder if kissing her would still feel and taste the same. If he thought she looked beautiful the first time they met, he simply was gobsmacked seeing her tonight. It felt like somebody had just hit him in the head; she was obviously way out of his league.

Caty let go of his tie, and he felt as if he was falling backward. She flashed a smile, and he silently cursed the gods for making him feel unprepared again. "Do you mean to say that if I ask you to do something for me, you'd do it, without any questions?"

"You want me to steal liquor."

"God, no," she exclaimed. "I'm not gonna ask you to do anything illegal."

He gave her a look, and she returned it, as if challenging him on who could play tougher.

"I just need you to act."

He panicked. Was there supposed to be some kind of show at this party that he didn't know about? Wasn't it just dinner and drinks and dancing?

"Just say yes."

"I don't know."

"Elan," she finally said his name, and he liked the way she said it. She remembered. She didn't dismiss him, after all. "Redeeming yourself, remember?"

"I was thinking of other ways."

She squinted her eyes. "Well, I want it to be *this* way."

Elan didn't speak. He simply pressed his lips together and smiled.

Caty sighed again, as if giving up. "Do this for me, please? If you do, all is forgiven. I'll even let you chase after Juliana all you want."

His forehead creased. "I won't do that."

"*Please, please, please.*"

"Well," Elan exhaled, "now that you've said the magic word."

Caty grinned, lifted her hand, and offered it. He took it and watched their fingers interlace. "All you have to do is pretend you are absolutely, mind-blowingly smitten with me."

He leaned forward as if pretending that he couldn't hear her through the music. His lips almost touched her cheek as he whispered in her ear, "That shouldn't be a problem."

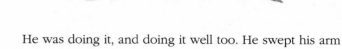

He was doing it, and doing it well too. He swept his arm up and circled her waist as they walked around the room, pausing every time Caty recognized someone. The chats were quick, and he picked up what he could from what she was telling people: what life was like in Toronto, how her mother was doing (even when they already knew, since her mother was in the same room), how her job was going, and a few snide remarks.

Caty was laughing, her spirits higher than usual, and she sometimes squeezed his rib. After a couple of times, he realized that she did this when she was uncomfortable answering a question, and it happened more than once. When he felt the squeeze, he jumped into the conversation, and she rewarded him with a tap, a secret conversation they were having in front of everyone.

Elan recognized a face in the crowd; it was Sarge Reynoso, someone he'd only seen on television but who was now in the same room as him, surrounded by people.

When they passed him, Caty kept walking, but Sarge was quick to call out to her.

She flashed a smile. "Mr. Reynoso, always a pleasure to see you."

"Hello, Catalina. I see you brought someone."

"Oh no, I just picked him up a second ago," she retorted.

Sarge guffawed in return. "You were always so funny. And so honest." He turned to Elan and declared, "Isn't she marvelous?"

Before Elan could answer, Sarge had moved on to his next question, "Who are you? I've never seen you before."

"I'm a friend of Juliana's." His default answer, the only one he could think of on the spot.

"Oh. Our prodigal daughter, Juliana. Did you meet in the city?"

"Yes, sir. In law school."

"Ah, so you're a lawyer like our Jules," Sarge went on, "and have you fallen in love with our little town as well?"

Elan couldn't answer right away. Had he? He had spent a lot of time there this year. "I guess so."

Sarge clapped his back and cackled, "Hard not to. We have beautiful heritage houses, all carefully restored. Good food, good liquor. A bunch of interesting people."

"Like you?" Caty jumped in.

Sarge smiled. "Why, thank you, young lady."

"Anyway," she continued, "we should head over to—"

"And what kind of work have you been doing? Are you saving trees like Juliana?" Sarge asked Elan.

Elan laughed at the way he reduced Jules's work to that—saving trees. In fact, she was doing much, much more.

"No, sir," he answered. "But I did plant a couple of trees for a volunteer mission."

"Isn't he great?" Caty pulled at him, eager for an exit.

Sarge opened his mouth to talk more, but Caty hurried on, leaving Elan to raise his hand goodbye.

They crossed the ballroom from one end to the other.

"Hey," Elan took a big stride and grabbed her arm.

She turned and asked, "We can still sneak out like you said, right?"

He paused and frowned at her expression. She looked upset, and he wondered what had happened in between that changed her. "I don't know what happened there."

She waved her hand. "It was nothing. I don't like talking to him. He likes to pretend he knows everything about everyone."

So Sarge Reynoso was a sore spot for Caty.

"Everyone's been giving me the side-eye since I arrived," she said.

Elan looked around and reported, "No one's giving you the side-eye. They may be looking at you, but come on. You showed up looking like an Oscar."

"An Oscar?"

"Yeah," he raised both his hands to illustrate a tiny trophy.

"You're telling me that I look like the Oscar, not that I look like I was attending the Academy Awards?"

Elan thought about it and said, "Yeah, that may sound better. But you are the fucking Oscar."

"The Oscar is a figure of a man," Caty pointed out, putting her hands on her hips, as if striking a pose. It was distracting.

"It's one of the most coveted things in the world," he argued. "I mean, if you're in that business."

Caty took her hands off her hips. "Oh. Well, if you put it that way."

"Who have you been watching?"

That took her off guard. "What do you mean?"

Elan looked around and found a table filled with couples, not all of the same age group. "All night, you've been looking back over your shoulder, craning your neck—"

"I have not." She started walking again.

He squinted at the table to get a better look, trying to figure out whom she was watching. Maybe he could just find Jules and ask her. Then his eyes met those of a woman at the table, and it took him a second to recognize her.

Elan turned around and looked for Caty, but she was already far ahead. He sprinted, avoiding people to catch up to her.

"It's *her.*"

"It's her what?" She didn't look at him.

"The girl from the day we met. When I dropped you off."

She came to a full stop, and her eyes bored into him. "You remember that?"

"Sure."

"What else do you remember?"

"I remember you not telling me what it was about."

Caty's voice was clipped. "Good. That's good memory."

She then proceeded to the bar.

"Are we making her jealous?"

She snorted. "Please. You're cute, sure. But I'm afraid she's married."

Elan craned his neck to look back at the table. "Then why are you making me do this?"

"You can stop doing it. It was an experiment. It didn't work. You are free to go around and follow Juliana as much as you like. You won't hear a thing from me. I am a hypocrite, and I know what you're doing too well."

He scowled. *This,* again. Is that what she really thought he was doing? Just following Jules around? He'd been sticking with Caty all night.

She took a shot glass from the waiter behind the bar and thanked him. She was about to down it when she paused to look at Elan. "You want one?"

"What is it?" He eyed the glass filled with clear liquid.

"This is the strong stuff, Judy. Don't drink it if you want to function tomorrow."

"Don't you need to function tomorrow?"

She raised a finger and shook it. "This doesn't apply to the pros."

Caty raised the glass and finished the drink. She set the glass down and hissed, "Oh yeah. This isn't for amateurs, Judy. Stick to the wine."

"How about we don't drink for a while?"

She rolled her eyes. "A party isn't fun without a little kick. This is the only way I can start laughing at these people who kept digging up bones in my closet."

Elan didn't say anything. He just waited.

"So what do you do, since Sarge already asked you?"

"Really?"

Caty rolled her eyes, "Yes, really. The other time, you asked me what I do."

"Right." He remembered. "Prop styling. How's that working out for you?"

"Really good memory."

"I survived law school," he smiled. "Family law."

Her nose scrunched, "Sounds boring."

"Well, someone's got to fix family squabbles. Sometimes, the best person is an outsider."

She pressed her lips and nodded, "That is so true."

Caty took a deep breath and then exhaled. "I feel warm all over now." She raised her hand and pulled her hair back. He noted that she seemed flushed from the liquor.

"Let me get you a glass of water." He walked over and crossed to the other side of the bar. No one was manning it seriously anyway, with most of the waiters on the floor carrying trays of entrées and wine.

Caty turned and asked, "Are you and my brother friends?"

"I guess?"

She smirked, "You're not sure?"

"I mean, we are. Yeah," Elan nodded.

"What else did you hear about me from the town?"

That was a weird jump to another topic, but he could tell this was something that bothered her. "Nothing much, why?"

"You already know about the summer before I left for Toronto?"

Elan remembered what Jules had told him a couple of months ago. It was one of those conversations where Caty's name was dropped, but it wasn't truly about her. It was about the accident that happened when Jules was still a teenager. Caty, Jules, and another friend went for a drive and got into an accident. It was the reason why Jules was so secretive when they first met—she was carrying a burden and had only let it go recently.

"Jules told me a little bit about it, yeah."

She frowned. Elan blinked, waiting for an answer she wasn't giving. So he poured water into a glass and handed it to her.

He watched while she drank, biding her time before the silence stretched on for too long. Someone should be changing the subject, but Elan wasn't budging.

Her eyes squinted, "Well. It was my fault. I was driving without a license. I was a minor. I hit someone."

His jaw tightened, and he reached for her glass to refill it.

"She died."

Elan sighed, "No, she didn't. She was hurt; you didn't kill anyone."

Caty leaned back, impressed that he knew that much. "Okay, so maybe you do know things. What else do you know about me? What else did they tell you?"

Elan shook his head. "Why would you say that about killing her?"

"People believe that shit, you know."

"I don't."

She paused, then she said, "Good, you shouldn't believe most of what they say anyway. They've said worse things about me."

Her words were jumbled, as if she was hurrying to get it out, to make it in time before the window closed.

"Worse than killing someone?"

Caty laughed. "Maybe that's the worst."

He smiled at how she still laughed, even if he was starting to realize that the gossip bothered her, and she cared a lot. She was in a room filled with people who thought badly of her, or at least she believed they did. Maybe that was why she kept looking over her shoulder. But there was another puzzle. "What's the story behind that girl who chased you?"

She scrunched up her nose, "Man, you're not gonna let that go, are you?"

"Fuck no."

"You're really getting the hang of cursing in front of me."

"You don't like it?"

"Jeez, Judy, I'm a lady." Caty leaned her elbows on the bar. "I love it."

He smirked, but he was determined. "Don't distract me. Answer the question."

"Fine. She's married to this guy. He's my dad's friend. We . . . uh. Whatever. Fine. I was in love with him."

"How old were you?"

She looked away. "I knew what I was doing."

"Okay, but did *he* know what he was doing?" Elan frowned, looking back at the table. Caty raised her hand, snapping her fingers in front of his face, "Hey, Captain Obvious. Stop."

"Are you telling me that you were in a relationship with someone much older than you when you were—"

"Oh, come on. I had a crush on him as a teen, that's all. Nothing happened 'til later on."

"But he encouraged it?"

Caty paused.

"Which one is he?" He tapped her hand away to get a good look at the table.

"I'm not gonna tell you."

"The bald one?"

"Excuse me. He's really good-looking." Caty looked back. Elan followed her gaze and saw a man sitting next to the woman he recognized. He was laughing and talking to everyone at the table. He barely noticed Caty looking at him. *The idiot.*

Elan cleared his throat. "Fine. He kinda looks like that guy. From the Bond movies. Not the new one."

"Pierce Brosnan?" She turned back, as if checking it for herself, but all it did was confirm whom she was watching.

"No, Connery."

Her jaw dropped. "I know you meant that as an insult, but how dare you! Sean Connery is hot."

"I mean, sure, that's your type." He was kidding of course, but she was laughing with him now, and he was mesmerized by the sound of it, loved that it was because of him.

"Oh my God, he's not even that old. You're the worst," she said, wiping her eyes as her laughter subsided.

She took a long look at him before smiling. "I'm glad you're here, Judy."

"Oh, no, no, no," Elan shook his head. "That story wasn't done. Tell me what happened with this guy."

"Nothing," she replied.

He gave her a look.

"Nothing, I mean it," she insisted. "I came home for a short while, we met, we had this fling. It ran its course. I went back to Toronto, and he married her instead."

He didn't say anything, but he could tell she had more to say.

"I should have been her, that's all. I shouldn't think that way, but I can't help it. I felt replaced, and I didn't like it. Also, I was the last to know, so imagine coming back home to that.

"It feels odd to say that out loud," she added, then groaned. "Everything sounds petty when you say it out loud."

"But you're not her." He handed the full glass back to her.

Caty hissed, "I believe I was already rubbing it in, don't need help on that."

"What were you trying to do with me then?"

She took the glass and held it close to her mouth. "I don't know. He hasn't looked at me this whole night. Hasn't even tried to contact me since I came home. I thought if I had someone drooling all over me, he'd at least spare me a second. I'm so annoyed. I'm not sure if I'm more annoyed at myself for caring or with him for not."

Elan looked behind her, straight to the table where he saw the man staring back at them. Elan's fingers curled, and his hand turned into a fist before he grabbed her shot glass. The bottle was just sitting there, so he took it.

Caty watched him. "Judy. I'm warning you."

He restrained his laugh as he poured. He raised the glass to her. "Just so we're even."

Elan tipped the glass and felt the liquid pass through his mouth to his throat. It didn't take long before he felt it burn straight to his stomach. He stammered, "Goddamn. Shit."

"It's the town specialty."

"You let people drink this?" He cleared his throat.

Caty smiled. "No, we only give this to the ones we want to stay for a while."

"Why?" Elan tilted his head, letting the burn settle. He sensed Caty watching him with absolute glee, and it made him feel a little better about drinking the shot.

"Okay." He clapped his hands when he felt good enough to get things going again. "Let's do it properly this time. I wasn't sure what I was doing earlier. But now I am."

"Do what?"

"Make him regret not choosing you."

seven

Who knew that stepping in as his sister's dance partner would finally pay off? Gia brought Elan to her dance class when they were kids because there weren't enough boys enrolled. Boys were mostly doing other things like guitar lessons, basketball clinic, karate, etc. Elan chose to do nothing for the summer, simply because he wanted to watch TV all day and play outside.

But Gia dragged him to dance class every Tuesday and Thursday. He couldn't say no, because their mother asked him to do it.

Gia wanted to be a part of Dancesport ever since she'd seen that movie with Patrick Swayze. Elan thought it'd be cool if he could start lifting girls from his sister's class like Swayze did in the movie, but then he glanced at his reflection in the studio mirrors and knew it was a long shot.

He did go through with the classes for the whole summer, though. Gia was a good dancer, and surprisingly, Elan wasn't that bad either. He didn't step on her toes. He was able to understand the steps and remember them.

Gia's dream only lasted for that summer, but Elan never forgot the dancing. He wasn't Dancesport material, but he knew how to lead.

"What are we doing? Wait, what are we doing?" Caty tugged at his arm as he walked ahead of her. He had drunk the poisonous drink that was the town delicacy, and it was spreading heat throughout his body.

"They told me you dance." He turned around.

She blinked. "When I was younger, yeah. Wait, they told you that? What else do you know?"

"Things," Elan answered as he offered her his hand. "We'll take it slow—just follow my lead."

Caty looked at his hand, then back at him. Her jaw dropped. "Oh my God. *You dance.*"

He eyed the couples already on the dance floor. "Only when needed."

She smiled and took his hand. "Am I even wearing the right dress for this?"

"You're wearing the perfect one." He stepped to her side, his hand still holding hers. Elan raised an eyebrow, willing her to walk with him. He didn't want to make her think this was a big deal—it was just dancing.

The room had been playing big-band tunes, and, at that moment, Elan actually knew what was playing. He even liked the Ray Charles song.

Caty took her first step, eyes glued on him, waiting for him to make the next move. They walked to the middle of the dance floor. Then he stretched out his hands, feet apart, and told her, "Twirl."

She hesitated for a beat but did what he said. Caty rolled to her side, and his arms enveloped her as she reached him. He caught her by the waist before her other hand landed on his. Although she wasn't facing him, Elan caught a glimpse of her smile as she turned.

The main thing he'd picked up from those classes was that girls love to twirl. So he made her do it again, on the other side. Caty turned with more confidence the second time, landing in front of him perfectly, arm hooked on his neck as she faced him.

Caty's hand found its place on his shoulder while his hand slid down her back. Her skin was warm, and so was her smile.

"Ready?" Elan asked.

"Good warm-up," she nodded.

"Give me your hand."

Caty took her right hand off his shoulder; he kept his hand on her back.

"Oh, this is serious dancing," she teased.

Elan moved his left foot forward, and Caty responded by putting her right foot back. The fact that they hadn't danced together before was obvious—there were hesitations and pauses—but they were quick to react to each other.

He stepped to the side, leading her to the right slightly. Her eyes widened, taking in the change of movement, and when he closed his right foot to meet his left, she completed the step by turning her body.

He heard her giggle. The sound of it made his stomach flutter, and he grinned. They continued down the length of the dance floor and knew that people were aware of them. Some paused to watch; some continued to dance and tried to keep up with them.

But Caty and Elan weren't paying attention. They were sizing each other up. Whatever Elan dished out, Caty was able to catch, her body movements fluid. She was like molten metal melding to his body, deliberate yet tender.

During the promenade, he made her turn again, and when she came back to face him, Caty leaned her head on Elan's shoulder and whispered, "Show-off."

She was enjoying it all; he could tell. He had never seen her smile this much. She had a glow around her, and it made her eyes sparkle.

"Wanna take a dip?" He took another step forward.

"Do I ever."

Elan took a side step, bending his other knee. He rotated his frame to the left, giving Caty the space to turn, angling her body to show her off. Her hair fell, exposing her shoulders and neck, and it took him an extra painstaking second before he pulled her back up.

Her chest heaved to catch her breath, the tip of her nose touching his neck. Elan breathed and finally took in the room. All eyes were on them.

No, all eyes on Caty.

He closed his eyes and heard her ask, "Is Otto looking?"

Somebody just stab me in the gut, Elan thought. That might have been better than what she had asked, but he opened his eyes and leaned back to look at her face. He didn't even check before answering, "Yes."

He knew. Any man would be an idiot not to be looking at her. He was surprised she'd even asked the question.

"And?"

Elan finally dared to look over at the table. His eye caught Otto's, and he saw the man frown before he turned away, his wife in tow. "I think he's leaving."

She laughed, the sound of it tickling his ear. Elan slowly turned back to her and saw the look of triumph on her face. "Who else is looking?"

"Pretty much everyone."

Caty's hand slipped from his shoulders to his chest. She took a second before she admitted, "That was the most fun I've had tonight. Most fun I've had here."

He grinned. That was a win. Not just for her but for him.

"Now, don't get any ideas," Caty had to say as soon as she stepped inside his hotel room. It was her disclaimer, and she felt silly saying it out loud. "I just don't like public restrooms."

Elan shrugged, closing the door behind him. Caty knew what she'd said earlier. They wouldn't do anything like the first time they met, but the circumstances were looking a little too similar.

She's not staying here tonight, no. She was just using the restroom to freshen up. The party wasn't even over yet. Her mother was downstairs, and so was her brother—with Juliana, whom Elan had been pining for.

She would never stay in his room tonight.

She didn't want to be talked about, and as much as she liked attention, she only wanted it when favorable.

And speaking of being talked about, she was dying to know more about what Elan revealed earlier. "What else did the town tell you about me?"

He snorted. "It really bothers you."

"Well, of course."

Elan pointed to the door. "I thought you needed to use the restroom."

She spun around. "I do. But I'd still like to ask you those questions when I'm done."

He nodded before she closed the door. She was lucky she got to close it before the smile spread across her face. She couldn't do a thing to stop it.

It was just everything—the way the night had turned out. She'd had high hopes for it, and it was coming true. Not in any way she'd imagined, but it was still welcome.

Caty looked at herself in the mirror and thought she looked a bit drunk. Not passed-out drunk but happy drunk. She tried to press her lips together, but she couldn't contain the smile.

Holy camoly, it had been so long since she felt as if she'd won something. Finally. Earlier, she hadn't realized how Otto deliberately led her on until Elan threw the fact out there. It was a revelation, something that validated her anger toward Otto. *The prick.*

And then, suddenly, it wasn't about him anymore. It was that she had asserted herself and conquered something today.

She looked at the mirror to check her appearance and ruffled her hair before going back out. Elan sat on the edge of the bed, coat off, loosening his tie. When she appeared, he looked up at her and smiled.

"I took ballet, quit, did different dances every summer," she started, jumping right in. "I played around with the genres. Might have quit a couple of times."

"They didn't tell me that much," Elan answered. "And then?"

She shrugged, "Then I just . . . stopped."

"Why?"

Caty sighed, "Well, I moved."

"Right," Elan nodded.

"What else do you know?" Caty had to ask. It felt unfair that he was getting bits of her from outsiders, especially if the sources were unreliable.

"Nothing as important as what I'd like to hear from you," Elan said, and it sounded like the closing statement of the interrogation she was just starting.

She closed her mouth and settled for a smile.

Elan looked at her intently, eyes never leaving her, and she replayed the words he had said all night: *You look great. I wasn't complaining. You're the fucking Oscar.*

It had happened during the twirl earlier, when he caught her back in his arms—she gasped, feeling a spark ignite within her. She thought she saw that fire in his eyes too, when his hand gripped her tightly to him.

But this was Elan. They had been on this road before. Plus, she'd already decided that fooling around with him again was a bad idea. Proven and tested.

She shook her head to rinse her mind of the humiliating memory. If Caty didn't enjoy being around Elan so much, she probably would have just avoided him. She was good at pushing people away, and she certainly could have done that to him.

But the kissing hadn't been so bad. Okay, so maybe she was holding on to that instead. Ironically, it had become a benchmark for other boys she kissed now. That doorway kiss was something else; she couldn't deny that, even though it ended the way it did. And that airport kiss?

Elan's eyebrows raised. "What are you thinking about?"

She knew she was turning red; she was positive. Caty straightened her back and lied, "Just how we must have looked on the dance floor."

"I'm sure you'll hear about it tomorrow."

She cringed, "God, you're right. They're gonna talk about us."

"I don't mind."

"Hmm," Caty tilted her head. She knew the town would talk, but she thought this night wouldn't show her in a bad light. At least that's what she hoped. "Well, I'm not gonna be here long enough to hear most of it."

Elan froze. His eyes blinked. "You're leaving."

Caty forced a smile, "Yeah. I still don't live here. I'm not planning to, ever."

He relaxed, "I just didn't know you'd be leaving so soon."

"I've got a couple of days. But you don't live here either," she pointed out.

He didn't say anything. He watched as Caty approached and sat next to him on the bed.

"So is it okay for me to ask you about the accident that night?" His eyes swept over to her. "I only really know what Jules told me and what you said earlier."

"Sure, what do you want to know?" she asked, although part of her didn't want to think about it. She spent a lot of time avoiding the memory. She hid it because no matter how many people tried to make her feel better, she still felt bad.

Her family dealt with the accident discreetly, kept it a secret from the town. It was hard considering that everyone knew everybody else's business, so they decided to fly her to Toronto for a fresh start.

She felt guilty, even though her therapist had told her these things happen. Bad things happen to people all the time. But despite that, she felt terribly alone after the incident, especially when they asked her to move to a new place. They kept telling her it wasn't a punishment for what happened, but it felt as if it was.

Nobody told her how it would be to feel so alone even when she was surrounded by people who were supposed to be there for her. The weight of her guilt rested on her shoulders, and it exhausted her.

"Do you still think about it?"

Caty paused, mouth slightly open. She took a quick breath before smiling. "Nobody has asked me that question before."

"Do you?"

"Yes," she nodded, "I try not to. It's not a pleasant memory."

"And you don't like talking about it?"

She mused. "I'm not gonna lie. I don't. We're all pretty hush-hush about it. It's just been catching up with me recently."

"Is that why you got weird with Sarge earlier?"

Caty laughed, "We're all weird with Sarge. The man thinks he's above us all just because he was in a soap opera and he used to go out with Marilyn Castro."

Elan snickered.

"Did they tell you that I did it intentionally—the accident?"

"No," he answered, straightening his back. "I didn't get the story from the others. I heard it from Jules."

"Oh," she sighed. "You know I could have. Done it intentionally."

He made a small smile. "Well, did you?"

She squinted. "I can't trust you. You're not my lawyer."

"You didn't do it," Elan concluded. It was possibly the best thing he could say at the moment.

"Nice of you to think that, but what do we do now?"

Elan shrugged. Caty put a hand on his shoulders, "What did I tell you about shrugging, Judy."

He let out a laugh.

"And you've been doing so well all night too," she continued. "The dancing was an excellent touch. Any other skills you've been hiding from me?"

"Plenty," he answered without hesitation.

Caty's eyes widened, and she leaned in closer to him. "Show me."

"No," Elan shook his head. "Best you just discover them over time."

Caty smiled, positioning her chin on his shoulder, their faces close enough to remind her of how they had kissed before.

Briefly.

"Are we becoming friends?"

"Thought we already were." Elan's brows met. "In some way."

Caty leaned back. "Mmm. Maybe you're right. See, not having sex made us friends."

She had to bring it up. They were in bed, again, and the last time that happened, it turned out badly.

He cleared his throat. "You think if we'd done it then, you wouldn't be with me tonight?"

"You mean, if it wasn't good?

"Oh, it would have been good."

"Cocky." Caty side-eyed him. "For someone who said he couldn't do it."

He bowed his head and let out a laugh. "For the record, I can; I just didn't know if I should then."

"Because of Juliana?"

He hesitated, she noted, before he nodded.

"It's okay," Caty sighed. "I like that we're friends. I don't have a lot of guy friends."

"Why not?"

"They cross the line most of the time," she answered honestly.

"Didn't we cross the line?"

"Barely," she scoffed. "We just kissed. Saw each other almost naked. Touched stuff. Okay, we did. But we weren't friends then."

He laughed but didn't add anything.

"Are you gonna ask me about, you know, what happened tonight with Otto?"

He looked already bored with the possibility of discussing it. He didn't like Otto, she could tell that much. "Do you want me to?"

Caty smiled. "I'm asking you."

He shook his head. "As far as I'm concerned, that's over. Am I wrong?"

"No." Suddenly she realized that he was exactly right. "It's most definitely over."

"I did note your use of the past tense when you told me how you felt about him."

"Did you?" She leaned back, raised her legs to the bed to make herself more comfortable.

"I get it. Just because you miss someone doesn't mean you want them back," he said.

"Are we talking about someone else now?"

Elan smiled. "No, we're still talking about you."

"I don't really miss him," she sighed. "I miss being wanted the way he wanted me. Which is wrong, because I think he never really wanted me. He just strung me along. I was young, so I didn't know better."

He grimaced, tugged on his tie in an attempt to remove it.

"You look cute when you're annoyed."

"I'm not."

She leaned forward and removed his tie for him. "Hmm, we've covered this before."

His hand touched hers for a moment before she laid the tie down.

Caty cleared her throat. "Let's talk about you now."

"Me?"

"What's your damage?"

Elan laughed. "You think I'm damaged?"

"Please. We're all damaged." Caty rolled her eyes as if this was all true and supported by facts. "I'm trying to figure out what's wrong with you."

"Well, thanks," he said in a monotone.

"Don't take that the wrong way." Caty took one of the pillows and laid it on her lap. "I like you."

"You have an odd way of expressing it."

"Anyway, since you've heard stories about me from this town, why don't you tell me some stories about you? So we're at least even?"

"My stories aren't as exciting as yours." He offered to take off her shoes, and she accepted.

"I don't care," she whispered. "You owe me the stories."

Elan smiled and watched her scoot down to rest her head on the pillow, hands folded over her belly. He wrapped his hands around her ankles, and she sighed with contentment at the warmth of it.

"I can talk to you about some cases I've read about instead."

Her eyes widened. "And tell me about how wretched people are?"

He started to rub her tired feet. Caty smiled. "And maybe how they're mostly misunderstood?"

He ran a hand up to her calf. "There was a case about this teen. He was adopted. His parents were great. Well, at least on paper."

The bed was comfortable, and Caty realized how her feet ached because of the heels she'd been wearing. The thing he was doing to her feet, pressing and stroking them, made her want to sink farther down. She could live like this, she thought. *Being tended to. Touched and cared for.*

"He was their only child. The couple was a bit old. They couldn't have kids when they were younger and later on decided they wanted a child. So they adopted him."

Caty put a hand on her face. "Did his biological parents want him back?"

"No."

"He ran away to look for his real parents, like in telenovelas?"

He paused. She met his eyes, immediately missing the sensation of his hands on her ankle.

"He robbed the couple."

"Yikes."

"He killed them too."

Caty jolted, kicking Elan in the process, but he caught her foot and laughed. "Oh my God, why would you even tell me that?"

"And you wanted me to believe you intentionally hit someone with your car?"

She sat up. "You're horrible. I am so not having kids after that."

"You asked for a story."

"I meant a nice one!" Caty pouted. "How are you not disturbed?"

Elan simply raised his eyebrows and laughed nervously, but he said nothing. Caty hoped he would keep talking. She needed to know more about him, but he cleared his throat and looked back at her instead. "You just get used to it."

"I get it. You're attracted to messed up people. That's your drift."

"*You're* not messed up."

A smile slowly crept up her lips. "Can we talk about something else now?" she asked.

"Sure."

"Where did you learn to dance?"

"I tagged along to dance classes with my sister. She told me she'd wash the dishes for the entire summer if I did it. Totally worth it."

"You have a sister," Caty smiled, taking what she could get. She reminded herself that she'd only met Elan twice, and she knew very little about his life. But she was comfortable with him in the same way people who had shared important moments in their lives were.

Elan nodded.

"Any other siblings?"

"No, it's just us." He paused. "Are we doing this? We're talking about family?"

"What would we rather talk about?" She laid her head back down. "This bed's really comfortable, by the way."

"I'll mention that to the receptionist when I check out tomorrow."

"You're leaving too?"

"Yeah."

Caty sighed, "So, this is our thing? We only see each other for a day?"

"We didn't even make it a full day." He put her foot aside and crawled into the space next to her.

"Do you think if we spend more than a day together, one of us might turn up dead?" she asked.

"Are we talking homicide or freak accident?"

She laughed. "I don't know; were you planning to kill me all this time?"

"That's actually a question for you. You're the one who ran over someone."

She closed her mouth and stared at him.

"Too soon?" He glanced at her.

Caty poked him on the chest, and he caught her hand.

Elan continued, "I don't think so. You occasionally drive me insane, but I don't get the urge to strangle you."

"*Yet*," Caty snickered. "And some people like to be choked."

"Some people or you people?"

She side-eyed him again but didn't answer.

He shook his head and laughed. "See, when you do something like that, it makes me—"

"Want to strangle me? Already?"

"Kiss you," he interrupted, and it sounded almost like a sigh.

Caty held her breath.

"But it's not as frequent anymore. I've realized something tonight."

She held her breath, trying to understand what he meant. *Kiss you. But not as frequent anymore.* She felt her breath escape as she said, "What?"

"As much as I want you to shut up, I also want to keep listening to you talk."

He looked at her when he said this, and it made her drop her head back on the pillow. The words hung in the air, and her mind was still trying to catch up with what it all meant. "You must be confused."

"A little, but I like it."

Caty's eyes shifted to the ceiling, waiting for words to just fall out of the sky and into her mouth. She had to settle for a laugh, even if it sounded nervous. She felt him turn to face her.

"You've never heard me sing," Caty blurted out.

"No. Am I missing something?"

"Yeah," she nodded. "Might push you over to the wanting-me-to-shut-up edge."

Caty finally shifted, twisting on her side to face him. They looked at each other, neither one sure of what to say next. Elan closed his eyes, tilted his head, and started singing, "*You're looking kinda lonely, girl . . .*"

Caty's brows met in the middle, but her mouth turned upward. He was close to whispering, but she recognized the tone in his voice.

"*Would you like someone new to talk to? Ah yeah, all right . . .*"

He was singing. In bed, next to her. She couldn't remember who sang the song, but she knew it. Caty started laughing as he hummed the next part, pretty sure he'd forgotten the lyrics. She remembered the song and joined the humming. They made up lyrics until they reached the chorus.

Caty clapped her hands, finally remembering the lyrics. They both sang, "*Sharing the night together, oh yeah, sharing the night!*"

"Oh my God, who sang that song?"

Elan shrugged.

"This isn't on your special skills set," she decided.

"Neither is it on yours," he agreed, the smile still on his face. "I can hold a better tune than you."

"That's an exception to wanting to listen to me."

He pressed his lips together and just smiled.

Caty propped herself up and scooted closer to him. "But I think it's safe to say that I've grown on you."

Elan opened his eyes, rolled on his back, and faced the ceiling.

"Come on," she urged, her face nearing his.

He glanced at her. "I guess."

She hit his arm playfully before dropping her head back down on his shoulder. She couldn't stop smiling.

"What do you think's going on at the party?"

She felt his shoulders move up, and she lifted her hand to stop him.

Elan shifted his hand up to softly touch her hair. "I don't think we're missing out on anything there."

She nodded. She felt his hand move away from her head and back to his stomach. A warm heaviness came over her, and she appreciated how nice it was to be with someone in comfortable silence. She figured they needed this, even for a minute, before going back down to the chaos of the party.

"We could still sneak out," she yawned.

"Maybe later." He started humming again, a different song this time, and she told herself she could close her eyes to enjoy this moment. He didn't sound bad either; she found his voice sweet and soothing.

They could sneak out later. The night was still young.

Caty turned to her side, her forehead now leaning on his shoulder, her hand gripping his arm. She felt Elan shift, his quiet breath on top of her head.

She found it quick to forget about the rest.

There was a whirring. *Something*. His fingers moved, then his hands, until he slowly opened his eyes. It was morning. He could tell by the light trying to peek through the curtains. Elan squeezed his eyes shut and breathed. An inexplicable calm covered him like a blanket. He turned to his side, and his heart leaped when he found the bed empty.

The sheets were undone, unsmoothed, like someone jumped out and ran. He sat up too quickly and blinked, the heaviness of sleep still dragging his body down. He leaned back on the headboard, running his hands over his face.

He looked back to his right side and confirmed it. He was alone. When he went to sleep, he hadn't been. He had slept blissfully last night, holding the woman he'd waited a long time to see.

He shifted his position and felt something underneath him. He grabbed the piece of paper under his torso and saw the hotel logo and a scribble. It read:

I didn't want to wake you. You looked nice. You sort of reminded me of a poem. That sounds like a line, but it's real. I'd quote Rimbaud if I could. "Le Dormeur du Val." Google it. Or maybe not.

He turned the paper over and read the words and numbers scribbled on the back. *In case you ever find yourself on my side of town.* He turned the paper again, then back, and laughed.

She had given him her number.

Three

But isn't desire always the same,
whether the object is present or absent?

ROLAND BARTHES

ONE MONTH LATER

What would you do if there were zombies right at your door?

Get peashooters.

Har-har. I mean, real zombies.

There are real zombies?

Yes. They eat people. They're everywhere.

Well, I don't see any zombies here.

Not for long. They're traveling.

Well, if that's the case, what should I do once the zombies get here?

Get a panic room.

I heard they're expensive.

Give me your passcode so I can come get you.

What if I did, and then you turned out to be a zombie too?

There's that risk. Guess you'll just let me eat you.

Oh, Judy. If you want to make a dirty joke . . .

Wasn't supposed to be dirty.

Just me then? I'm the only one thinking about this?

Well, now that you've brought it up . . .

Call me in three minutes?

Can't. Still at work.

You can't call to say hi from work?

Are we just gonna say hi?

Are we gonna keep talking about zombies?

Nope.

Offer only stands for two minutes.

TWO MONTHS LATER

I haven't been sleeping well. I look like a zombie today.

Well, hello to you too.

Hey.

You okay?

I think I should get one of those noise machines. Listen to cicadas or something.

I didn't take you for a cicadas girl.

Don't I look like I like sleeping outdoors?

Do you like sleeping outdoors?

No. I hate bugs.

Cicadas are bugs.

That's why I need the noise machine. Not the outdoors.

Did you really wake me up to talk about cicadas?

Yes. Sorry. I forget that you exist in a different time zone.

Because I keep answering your messages anyway?

Exactly. What is wrong with you? Do you always have to answer?

That's funny.

Did you fall asleep?

Are you watching me just type things now?

Judy.

Fine, I'm going to talk to my friends about cicadas.

Photo attached: CICADA.JPG

WHAT THE HELL

THIS IS DISGUSTING

WHY WOULD YOU SEND ME THIS

That's a cicada.

I HATE YOU.

THREE MONTHS LATER

Judy >

Hey. Did you see the finale?

Not yet. No spoilers.

I didn't even see it yet.

Why not?

I dunno. Maybe over the weekend.

You can survive for days without people actually spoiling it for you?

Oh, I already know what's happening. We have a very loud intern.

Did you punish him?

Made him go through the archives to look for something that maybe doesn't exist.

You're a disgrace to human resources.

I'm so proud of you.

Watch the finale over the weekend?

My night, your night?

Whatever's better for you.

I can do Saturday morning. Wait, I think Lucian is throwing our Goodbye Suckers! party.

Already?

I can't stress enough how much we both want to tell everyone we're moving to New York.

Oh, you've stressed it to me plenty.

Saturday night?

What, no parties?

No, I'm going to stay in and snuggle with you.

Same time?

Same time works.

FOUR MONTHS LATER

Caty >

5:54 AM · 49%

Sorry I missed that text. I was running around all day.

How's the move?

Well, I got my last box.

Nothing broken?

Yeah, all good.

Good.

FIVE MONTHS LATER

Judy >

7:37 AM · 53%

Sorry, missed that call. I was in court.

No worries, I've got to water this guy's plant.

As a favor?

No, as his assistant, I'm expected to water his plants. Turns out, his former assistant killed a cactus, so I'm on probation until I get this plant to bloom. Who kills a cactus, really? You don't even have to water them.

It's possible to overwater it.

Well, excuse me, Mr. Cacti.

What happened to that job at the magazine you wanted?

I'm working on it. But for now, I have to water plants.

Don't overdo it.

Are you home now?

On my way. Just need to drop by somewhere.

Well, don't text and drive. I don't want you to die a tragic death just talking to me about the death of plants. Why are we talking about death so much?

I'm not gonna die.

Drive home. Sleep. Oh, when you can, text me cactus trivia.

For an assistant, you're extremely bossy.

This is temporary.

Of course it is.

SIX MONTHS LATER

ılll   6:21 AM   51% 🔋

<

Caty >

Hey. You there?

Hey. Yup, where else would I be?

I've got news for you. Don't know if it's good.

Did you finally resign as Jules's bitch boy? She's got my brother for that now.

Funny.

I'm hilarious. But news? Good? Bad?

You be the judge.

Shoot.

I have a conference to attend in Philly.

I can swing by New York after.

Silly man. You don't just swing by New York.

I could only swing by.

So that's your deal? You're a swinger now?

Caty.

You're coming to see me?

Lady Liberty first.

She's not even that pretty.

No contest. So? Good? Bad?

You're finally coming to see me.

We have a three-day conference.

Sure.

But I have some days off
after. So I can see you.

You don't have to attend your fake
conference. You can just see me right away.

I'm there for five days, and then I'm gone.

So a three-day conference
and two days of doing what?

Well, if you're taking me in, you're gonna
have the burden of thinking about that.

Two days. I guess we'll find out if we're
gonna end up killing each other after all.

eight

She usually drew the line at poetry. Caty read for leisure, to take her mind off certain things—like Elan coming to New York tomorrow. It's not a big deal. Except it's been six months since they last saw each other. Since they . . . slept together. Literally.

She was reading Neruda and trying not to think about that night. But sometimes, she came across things that brought her back. Certain conversations, songs, poems.

She finished the piece she was reading and had to close the book because she remembered so vividly. It was hell living on the memory of that one night.

Did she try to compare it to nights with other guys? She did. Did she stop going out with other guys and kissing them? Sure. She remembered the feeling she'd had when she woke up the next morning, finding that somehow she was still wrapped up in his arms. It was one of the most peaceful nights she'd had in a long time. Their limbs had found a way to stay tangled, as if they didn't want to separate themselves from each other.

The funniest thing was that nothing had even happened. She slept with someone. Maybe a real sleep, for the first time.

She remembered nights with other boys she'd been with before—they'd held her after, sure. But somehow, in the morning they would end up with their backs turned, almost at the edge of the bed.

Okay, Caty breathed. She was reading too much into that one night. She was being dramatic. It was fine. It was a good night. Nothing mind-blowing. The memory had more of a subtle feeling, like a tender rhythm that made her blush or curl her toes if she thought about it too much.

Really. *This.* Over sleeping.

Good God, get a grip.

The past few weeks hadn't been so great. She felt as if she was literally watching the most drawn-out morning after, but the first few months were admittedly cute. They were calling each other, texting nonstop, watching TV together over the phone. Now it just seemed *sad.*

She really should have known she was in too deep after a date with another guy on one of her first nights in New York. They were having a blast that night until he kissed her, and she thought, *I should check my phone for messages.*

Clearly, there was something wrong with her.

But, in fact, when she did check her phone after the guy leaned back and opened his apartment door for her, there was a message from Elan. It was so casual, so innocent—he had no idea where she was, what she was doing, whom she was with.

They couldn't seriously keep talking through their phones. She kept thinking something's got to give.

But tomorrow was different.

Tomorrow he would be in New York. *Her* New York. She felt her stomach flip at the thought of seeing him again. She was confused, because she wanted to see him so much that her chest just might burst open. Half of her dreaded the meeting, and half was desperate to see him.

Caty didn't know. She felt very much like the Jane Austen quote *I am half agony, half hope.* She needed to read something else. Not this. Not wanting. Not desire.

Her alarm went off, and she practically leaped out of her seat. She didn't even look at the reminder. She turned off the alarm, dropped her book, and got her purse.

She had to water some damn plants.

He didn't think he'd ever make it. New York. The one his old neighbors sang about during their late-night drinking and karaoke sessions. *New York, New York, the city that doesn't sleep.*

It was just before noon when he got off the brutal bus ride from Philly. His colleagues were probably in their hotel rooms, sleeping in before flying off tomorrow. Today was their free day. He wanted to have more days, or as long as his visa would allow him to stay, but it all depended on how today went.

No pressure at all, he kidded, but he'd like to think he was ready for it. He stepped off the bus and shook his head. *Nope.* He wouldn't let the pressure get to him today. He would not think about people on another continent. Especially since he'd been doing that for the last six months—thinking nonstop about a person who lived in another country. The same person walking toward him now.

Catalina. He had started calling her that in his head; it seemed more intimate, as if he knew her better than other people. She looked nervous.

Her hair was back to black, slightly curled at the ends, skimming below her shoulders. Her skin was bright, her eyes dark, her lips a more muted color than he'd seen before, but she looked beautiful, always. It was still summer in New York, but she wore dark clothes. Black top, black deconstructed jeans, black ankle boots.

There was a lot to take in—New York for one thing, with its streets and buildings and culture. Even the air smelled different here. Looking around, he noticed so many new things, but everything faded when she came into view. She took the last step toward him with a sigh. He smiled.

She looked up at him, and he expected her to say something, but she didn't. Instead, she smiled back, took another step closer, and he caught her in his arms.

He felt Caty's arms wrap around his neck, and his chin landed on her shoulders. She smelled like coffee, with a hint of the perfume she wore the first time he was this close to her.

They stayed like this on the sidewalk, not speaking, not moving. They just breathed in and out as people walked past them.

They were together. In New York. They had today. It seemed like a good idea to spend the first few minutes of it wrapped around each other.

Elan was here. He looked leaner, his hair was shorter, his jaw more pronounced. He had lines on his forehead when he looked at her, brows arching up.

When she let go of him, she suddenly didn't know what to do next. What to do with him. *He was here.*

Caty felt him watching her, so she said, "How was your fake conference?"

His face broke into a smile, and her insides hurt. "As good as fake conferences go."

"Happy to see me?"

"Always."

She stepped to his side and looped her arm through his. "Welcome to New York. The greatest place on Earth."

"I thought that was Disneyland."

Caty shook her head as they started to walk. "Nope. That's the happiest. This is the greatest, Judy. This is it."

She watched his face light up. The sun hit his eyes, so he squinted when he said, "Well, you're here, so it must be."

"Damn right."

They walked quietly for a bit, just moving forward, not exactly sure where they were heading.

"You're wearing black," Elan started.

She looked down at her clothes, then back at him, "Oh yeah. Grunge is back. Or maybe it never left. I'm having a phase."

"Since when?"

"Since moving," Caty answered. "It seems like the safest thing to wear."

"You mean like from pickpockets?" He frowned. "People harassing you?"

"God, no." She snorted. "Not like that. Though a guy flashed his penis at me the other day."

Elan looked funny. "On the street?"

"No, in the comforts of my own room," she clicked her tongue. He stiffened.

"I'm kidding!" Caty laughed. "But I live in Bed-Stuy, so I've been roughened up around the edges."

Elan smiled easily. "You have always been rough around the edges."

"It can get scary here at times, but if you don't let it roll off your back, you're gonna book the next flight out."

Elan nodded, and their steps slowed. "So. All black?"

Caty took a deep breath. "Newbie anxieties. Fitting in. Black seemed safe. And it looks good on me, don't you think?"

She looked up at him, watching him smile. God, she could do this now. See him smile. Not imagine it. Despite talking a lot the past few months, she now realized they had never done a video call. They were together in different ways for the whole time, but not in that sense. Introducing visuals would just be too weird, too much to ask for maybe. They were doing fine talking in speech bubbles and voice clips. Now that she could scan his face, memorize the way his cheeks stretched and his eyes wrinkled, she realized she'd been missing out.

"I never took you for someone who'd go for safe just to fit in. Weren't you the girl who liked to shock people?"

Caty smiled. "Yes, well. I want New York to actually like me. I feel brand new here."

New York felt more like a clean slate than Toronto. New York was her choice; Toronto, even when her parents insisted otherwise, felt like her punishment.

He didn't say anything more, just nodded and looked at the streets. He was taking it all in, she figured. The signs, the stores, the people, the cabs. She had done exactly the same thing when she arrived, and it finally dawned on her that she was actually living in New York.

"So where do you get your bagels here?"

She grinned. *Bagels*. He remembered—her choice of breakfast. She covered her mouth and squealed. "You want bagels?"

"No, *you* want bagels."

"Well, what do you want?"

He put a hand on the small of her back, and they resumed walking. "Don't mind me. I'll just follow you around."

"No, there must be something you want to see, right?"

Elan just grinned.

"We'll pay a visit to your lover, Lady Liberty."

"Yes." He fisted his hand and thrust it into the air, like that iconic Judd Nelson move.

She laughed. "But I mean, the best things are in Brooklyn." She reached for his arm. "I might need to reroute this whole thing. Are you up for it?"

His hand wrapped around her wrist, and she responded by turning it so her fingers could touch his.

"Up for it? I came prepared."

He used his other hand to pull a piece of paper from his pocket and handed it over to her. Caty took it and read the scribbled words. She paused, her eyes running down the list, and then looked back at him. "Are you serious?"

"It's all you've talked about."

She laughed, looking back at the list of places she'd been visiting for the last two months since moving to New York. It wasn't even the tourist spots; these were places she'd mentioned because she liked them—the vintage shop in Brooklyn, Franklin Park, DUMBO at night. They might not be able to cover everything, but she squeezed his hand and tried hard not to giggle.

"Lead the way," he said, as she leaned in.

Caty pressed her lips together and tried to stop herself from saying the things she wanted to say. *Too early.* They had two days. They could talk about it, whatever it is, later.

"That all you have?" She pointed to his bag.

"I had one of the guys take most of my stuff home so I wouldn't have to bring everything here."

Caty nodded. "You're a light packer. I could never stay for two days with one bag."

Elan paused. She saw his jaw twitch, and her stomach twinged. But he took a breath, and his face shifted, back to the way it was when they held hands, like things were back on track. "Well, I didn't bring a suit this time. Do I need one?"

Caty bit her lip, remembering the last time they saw each other. The ball. The dance. The room. The bed. The morning after.

She cleared her throat. "No. You look fine. Great, even."

"Thanks." He smiled and stepped forward, as if he knew where they were and where they were going.

But he didn't. He was an outsider. Caty looked down at her feet and thought she probably seemed the same. She did know these streets and which way to go, but since moving here she'd never felt more like she was with somebody who was just like her.

nine

She was talking to the guy at the customer service desk when his phone rang. He saw his sister's name and hesitated to answer. She'd understand. She knew he was in New York, and he had told her why.

But that only made him worry more. Since Gia knew about Caty, she must be calling for an important reason. His hand hovered over the screen, contemplating, but she dropped the call.

She must have forgotten, Elan thought. She could text him if she really needed something.

They were at Spoonbill & Sugartown Booksellers because it was on the list. The bookstore was one of the first places she'd visited in New York as a teenager.

He stared blankly at the books in front of him until she returned. "Any luck?"

"No," she answered. She was looking for a certain book, and it wasn't on the shelves. Caty peered at the shelf in front of him. "Anything you're looking for?"

"Actually . . ." Elan stretched his hand out and grabbed a book with a red spine—*Arthur Rimbaud Complete Works.* "This is the same guy, right?"

"Same guy as what?"

"The one you mentioned in your note." Elan turned to her, holding the book.

She quickly looked down at her feet. "Which one?"

"You wrote me more than one?"

Caty snatched the book from him. "I told you to *google* it."

"You said maybe I shouldn't," he countered.

She rolled her eyes, opening the book. "You can do what you want, you know. You don't have to do everything I tell you."

He smiled, watched her run her hands down the table of contents. "So you want proof that poem actually exists? That I wasn't just making up excuses for leaving you that morning?"

"Hey, you said it."

She flipped the book open and handed it to him. "Of course it exists. If you must know, it's one of my favorites."

He was delighted that she was sharing her favorites with him, and now he would like to read the rest of the book, even if he didn't know a thing about poetry. She hadn't really talked about poetry when they were texting, just that she had read it. He wondered what more he could be missing since their time together was so limited. He took the book from her and read "Le Dormeur du Val" in French, then the translation on the next page. He had actually googled it and read it once or twice, but he really just wanted to bring it up with her now.

Elan felt Caty's eyes on him as he read on, and he took his time until he reached the very end. "Hmm."

"What?"

"You thought I looked dead."

Caty scrunched up her nose. "I knew you would say that."

And then there was that: a familiarity between them, and they knew each other well enough to guess each other's reactions. She'd known he would say that, and in turn, he knew how she would respond.

"You looked peaceful," she explained. "Ignore that last line."

"But that was the point of this whole poem."

"Okay . . . for you. But I liked the imagery, so that was the point of it for me."

Elan closed the book and placed it back on the shelf. "I thought the point of it was that you left me your number."

She smiled but quickly turned around. "Yeah, well. I've accepted the fact that you're not just Juliana's law school friend or Kip's friend or whatever. You're also . . ."

He caught up to her, just in time for her to say, "Mine."

Mine.

Elan paused and thought his smile expressed so much relief that it showed. Caty smiled back, hers more of joy than relief, and for a while everything stopped. Time and the world around them froze as they looked in each other's eyes.

Until his phone rang.

Caty quickly averted her eyes, "Oh hey, Lucian was looking for that book."

Elan watched Caty as the intimate moment disintegrated. But it wasn't her fault. It was the thing he was holding in his hands.

One missed call. Five messages.

Gia: Who's Mom's doctor again?

Gia: Where do you keep her papers?

Gia: Don't worry, she's fine, just taking her to the hospital.

Gia: Do you know if she's allergic to anything?

Gia: They've got her records here. We'll be okay. Sorry!

He stared at his phone for the longest time, reading the whole thread of messages. There must have been a delay.

He quickly dialed Gia's number for the answers. She hadn't even said what happened or what went wrong. Why was she taking their mom to the hospital?

But did it have to happen now, really? When he left, she was okay; she'd just had her routine checkup. What the hell happened while he was away?

The phone kept ringing, but Gia didn't answer. Elan sent texts asking her what had happened.

He looked up and saw Caty turning back to him, brows furrowed.

"You okay?"

Elan slid his phone back to his pocket, "Yeah."

He saw her hesitate, worry showing on her face before she said, "I'll just pay for this one, and then let's go to the next stop, okay?"

They were done. They had walked around the city, taking in the sights, talking about things they'd written about over the past six months and some that they hadn't. It was dark, and Caty's feet ached.

There were some places on Elan's list that they weren't able to cover considering the distance and their time, but there was one place that they knew they had to visit.

She was trying to decide whether she should introduce Elan to Lucian on this first night or if it was better to save it for the next—if there actually would be a next night. She wasn't so sure anymore. Everything was fine for the first few hours, but as the day dragged on, Elan seemed to be in a rush. He was insisting on meeting Lucian today. Maybe he was just nervous? Overwhelmed?

But Caty agreed it might be better to see Lucian the first night because she also really wanted the two to meet. She imagined it should be more of a lunch setting, though, with Lucian's boyfriend, Jimmy, but she'd talked so much about Riot! that of course it made his list. So here they were, in line at the front door.

"How are you with crowds?"

"Okay," Elan answered, "I live in the city too, you know."

Caty smiled. "Sure, but how are you with loud crowds?"

"I've had my share of public transportation in the Philippines; I think I can *definitely* handle crowds."

"Right."

Elan paused, eyeing her. "Does Lucian know I'm coming?"

"Yes, I told him. I even asked him to meet us for lunch tomorrow."

He hesitated. "You seem nervous."

Her eyes widened. She thought that was him, but of course, *duh*. He knew that she considered Lucian to be family, so this suddenly felt as big as meeting her parents. *This is meeting Lucian.*

"Promise you'll be cool with all of this?" Caty asked.

He looked at her, confused. "Why wouldn't I be?"

Caty blurted out, "You might get hit on by men taller than you. In full makeup and heels. And sparkly dresses."

She knew it would be a deal breaker if he turned out to be the guy who couldn't handle that. She had dropped men like flies the moment they said something remotely idiotic and rude about her friends.

It was a risk, because she already liked Elan so much, but every time she mentioned Lucian and Jimmy or Riot!, he seemed cool about it.

"I can't say that hasn't happened before, so it's okay." Elan smiled.

She nodded, took another step, and they found themselves right by the entrance. Caty simply flashed a smile at the bouncer—they were on a first-name basis—and stepped inside.

Caty loved Riot! because it was a place of freedom, love, and laughter.

She spotted Lux's big, blond hair right away. She was talking to friends in her usual way—loud, and a little bit obnoxious, but always fun. Caty let go of Elan's arm to wave and get her attention.

When Lux spotted them, she excused herself and made her way back to them. She was feeling her Britney Spears fantasy that night and wore her own interpretation of the iconic jewel-encrusted bodysuit Britney wore at the VMAs.

"Hi, Caty Cat." She leaned in to give Caty three kisses on the cheek, like the Dutch. One brow arched at the sight of Elan. "Who's the dish?"

Lux knew exactly who he was. Caty had only told her a hundred times. "This is Elan."

"Hi," Elan said with a smile.

Lux offered her hand, and he took it. They shook once. It would have been better if he kissed it, like Lux wanted, so she pursed her lips. "Well, if it isn't Caty's nap buddy. In the flesh."

Caty coughed and laughed it off. Elan straightened his back, then laughed. "I guess that's me."

Lux grinned, still gripping Elan's hand with both of hers. "What's wrong with you?"

Caty glanced at him to see his reaction. He looked a bit surprised by the question, so she jumped in. "Really? That's your first question?"

Lux ignored her and winked at Elan. "Mind you, you're not the only one she's had a nap with in this lifetime, but you're the one that stuck, I see."

"Really."

Caty shook her head. "The only one who got to meet the fabulous Lux."

Elan smiled. "Hey, that's nice."

"Not really." Lux shook her head, finally letting his hand go. She was tall and even taller with her seven-inch heels. "I've never met any of her men. She's scared that I'm gonna snatch them away. So what does that tell me about you?"

Elan shrugged.

Caty put a hand on his shoulder. *Habits,* she thought as she patted him. "Don't be sassy, Luxie. I like this one."

Lux put a hand on her hip and smirked, "So what are you fake love birds doing for tomorrow?"

That was the question, wasn't it? What were they going to do tomorrow and for all the hours they had left? She didn't want to think about it, but she had been counting the hours. Subtracting them from her assumed total.

So that's what had happened to her—she'd become the girl who counted the hours. She bit her nail and listened to Elan talk about where they'd been all day, how he loved the food trucks, and how they scoured Brooklyn Flea for the most random things.

She smiled while she listened, until she realized that she'd never walk around DUMBO again without thinking of Elan.

Lux noticed the change in her expression. "You all right, darling?"

She waved her hand. "Just a bit tired from all the walking."

"Let's find a seat," Elan suggested.

Lux smirked, "Relax, lover boy. She sits by the bar—her butt's basically embossed on it by now."

Caty laughed as they headed to the bar. She said hey to the bartenders and ordered a drink.

"You should go to a museum tomorrow," Lux suggested. "The tourists love that."

"I don't know," Caty shrugged. "We're gonna see how tonight goes. I just couldn't let him leave New York without seeing Riot!, and this might be his only night. I really don't know."

He'd never told her the exact time his flight was leaving, but she couldn't imagine having Elan for two nights. She just couldn't wrap her head around it.

"Well, you only need one, am I right?" Lux teased.

Elan caught that and grinned. He knew. He knew she talked about him with Lux and that they weren't just teasing him earlier.

Caty shook her head, telling her to stop.

"What?" Lux's eyes widened. "But just so you know, Elan, you can't just fly in and fly out of New York."

"I told him the exact same thing."

Elan laughed apologetically. "It is a shame."

"Mmm-hmm," was Lux's only reply.

"So I had to show him the best of the best right away, right?" Caty perked up.

"Welcome to Riot!" Lux raised her arms up, and the crowd cheered. "You might want to unbutton that shirt a bit—we don't do stuck-up here."

Caty giggled and eyed Elan's shirt. He laughed too, but he didn't unbutton it.

"I better jet," Lux said, blowing air-kisses to them both this time. "I'll see you on the other side."

Caty breathed deeply, taking in the energy of the room. There was cackling, sequins, and big hair. For her, being there was the closest thing to being with family.

Caty turned to Elan, and he took a deep breath too. "I like her."

"Wait 'til you meet Lucian," she smiled.

"That's not him?"

Caty grinned. "It is, it is. Lux, Lucian, one and the same. Lucian wears less makeup, though."

Elan nodded, and she could see that he was collecting all the information. Facts. Trivia. Images of her life here in his head. It felt as if she was being stripped naked, and not in the way she preferred. But she shook the thought out of her head and reminded herself that he'd only be here for a few more hours. She would make it as pleasing as he needed it to be. Caty looked over at his beer bottle. "You good? You want anything else?"

He cleared his throat. "Actually, I need to tell you something."

The lights dimmed, and Caty knew the show was starting. Her head whipped back to the stage. "Wait, it's starting."

"What is?"

A spotlight turned on the stage, revealing a lady wearing a black leather one-piece suit. She had her back turned, and the music started to play. Caty tapped his arm, eyes still fixed on the stage. "Only the most entertaining thing you'll ever see in your life."

Elan had never seen anything like it before. It was loud and hilarious and peculiar. And then there was Caty. She was fixated on the stage, her eyes lighting up, laughing at every punch line. Lux was onstage too now, lip synching a mash-up of Adele's "Rolling in the Deep" and then Britney Spears's "Toxic." She was easily one of the crowd's favorites, and she obviously loved the attention, exaggerating her moves every time they cheered.

When the show ended, Caty ran backstage, and he was left alone at the bar, politely nodding to everyone. They knew he was a newbie because they all seemed to recognize each other here, Caty included. When she returned to him, she was bubbly and bouncy.

"You okay?" she finally asked.

He nodded. He was. He was just . . . worried. She was having the best time, and he was about to tell her something disappointing. He really should have told her earlier. If she knew, they probably would have done things differently. Not that he didn't like what they had done. Walking around from place to place was fun, but he felt as if he needed to just have her in one place for a time so they could both settle.

"All right, next stop is on you. Where do you want to go next?"

"Really?"

"Yes, really."

"How about we just retire to my room?"

Caty leaned back. "Jeez, Grandpa."

"I have to fly out in the morning." Not the way he should have said that, but it was close to midnight, and he only had a couple of hours left. He knew that he should have said something to her when he decided to move his flight to an earlier one, but he screwed up. He couldn't hold off any longer, no matter how much he wanted to.

Elan watched her mouth open and eyes widen, giving away her shock.

"Emergency," he added. To explain why. To make his departure less rash. "I just found out this morning."

She blinked a couple of times before she shook her head. "Okay."

Elan winced, not sure what to do. Should he tell her more? But he couldn't. It was just too all over the place. He had already told her about some of these things. How there was only him, his sister, and his mother. How his mother had been getting sick recently. How much that had been bothering him.

She stumbled over the words, "I guess we should call it a night."

Elan thought she would say goodbye to her friends, but she started walking and went straight to the door and out to the street.

He caught up with her, nodding at people he'd been introduced to when they said goodbye, then tugged at her hand.

"Wait, that's not what I meant when I said we should retire to my room."

"Say *retire* one more time—" Caty looked back at him, finally. She had recovered and no longer seemed surprised or disappointed. Instead, she looked annoyed. "It's really not helping your case, Grandpa."

Elan decided he'd better do something. She had been pulling away since coming to Riot!, and he didn't know why. So he held on to her arms, pulled her in, and looked her in the eye. "What's going on?"

"What?"

"You've been avoiding me all night."

"Are you serious?" Her brows furrowed. "I was with you the entire time."

"Don't get me wrong, Riot! is great, but we can't even have a decent conversation in there."

"*You* wanted to go to Riot! *You* wanted to meet Lucian."

"I did. But just the whole day, we've been running around the city like we're in a rush—"

"It's New York! You wanted me to show you New York!"

"I wanted to see you."

He felt Caty soften, her shoulders slumping.

"Did you not have fun?" She stepped to his side, and he let his fingers slide away. "Didn't you like everything?

"I did." Elan watched her ease herself out of his hold. "That's not what I'm saying."

"Did you hate Riot!?"

"No," he said quickly, "that's not it at all. A couple of dudes hit on me, and I thought that was pretty good for my ego since my date couldn't look me in the eye."

Caty looked away and bit her lip in dismay. "It's not a date."

"You know what I mean," he sighed. His fingers tipped her chin up. "Hey, Caty. It's just me."

She moved away. "Let's just go."

ten

Caty came into the hotel when he checked in and walked up to the room with him. She knew she should have offered her apartment, but it was a small space for three people, and it certainly wasn't big enough to house the tension between them now.

Truthfully, she didn't want him to invade all of her space. She wanted to have something of New York to herself so when he left, she wouldn't associate it with him.

Plus, it might imply things, and she didn't want that either. She wanted to see how this day played out—without preconceived notions, if that was possible. But it was proving to be hard.

They hadn't spoken since leaving Riot! It wasn't a good silence. It was like that time he drove her to the hotel before she flew back to Toronto, only the tables had turned. She was the one who wasn't talking to him.

When he opened the door, she looked around and was relieved that it wasn't just a room with a bed. It was spacious enough to have a small receiving area with a desk, a couch, and a huge window that overlooked the city.

Elan went straight to the middle of the room while she stayed by the door, still not sure if she should stay or go. They stared at each other, waiting for the other to talk first.

"Are you gonna talk to me now?"

"I don't know," Caty shrugged. "When were you planning to tell me that you're leaving earlier?"

He nodded, as if he knew this was coming. As if he actually had an answer before she asked the question. "If it was possible, never."

Her eyes widened. *He actually said that?* That wasn't the answer she wanted.

"So you were just gonna leave without telling me? You were gonna disappear and then call me later and say, 'Oops, sorry, I flew back when you went home to shower,' or something?"

Elan sighed. "I don't know. I meant to tell you, but I couldn't."

"That doesn't make it okay."

"I know. I'm sorry. Again."

Caty walked over to the couch and slumped herself into it. She rubbed her cheeks with her palms before saying, "This sucks, Elan. I've been stressing about this the whole time."

He walked over to her carefully, then he took the other end of the couch. "I didn't want that to happen."

"It's just that *you're here*."

Elan tried to understand what she meant, but she wasn't explaining it very well. Explaining it would mean unloading the thoughts about the visit that littered up her mind. It was unfiltered and messy.

"This is weird," she admitted.

"Did it feel weird the entire time?"

"It didn't for you?" Caty looked at him, wide-eyed.

His jaw tightened as he looked away.

"I'm just not used to you being in my space," Caty explained, hoping it would soften the blow. She realized that sounded harsh and knew she wouldn't want to hear it if she was in his position. "For the entire time we've known each other, I've been the one invading yours."

He nodded, still quiet.

"Something's changed," she added, her voice almost a whisper.

Elan looked back, and she felt embarrassed. Her eyes focused on the carpet below her.

"What?" he asked.

Caty took a deep breath. "We've never had so much time together."

Out of the corner of her eye, she saw him smile, but it still didn't feel safe to look at him.

"Well, we were pretty preoccupied the other times too," Elan commented.

She smiled weakly for only a moment before she remembered that she felt awful, as if there was something in the pit of her stomach—an impending doom, disappointment.

He raised his brows, a nudge to keep her talking. She responded, "I just feel weird about it, that's all."

"Why do you feel weird around me now? We never had that problem before."

Caty exhaled. "I don't know. You don't feel weird around me?"

"No."

She squinted. "Really?"

He seemed so cool about it. "Really."

She got it now. She was the only one feeling weird about this because she was the only one whose feelings had changed. Sure, Elan might have disliked her the first time they met, but everyone did. She was used to that. She either grew on people and got close to them or she shut them out for good. Caty was fine with that.

But she'd started to think about Elan while reading love poems, woke up to dreams of him, kept him in her head on her way home from work. He was with her all the time, but that was nothing like having him *here* in the flesh, warm and gentle and tangible. Solid. A real presence. What she had settled for in the past few months was not even close to this.

He was here, close to her, fingers at the edge of the couch, just an inch away from her shoulders. She stood. "We're not strangers anymore."

It was true. Caty could honestly say that Elan knew about real pieces of her now—the things she revealed during their daily conversations. Even the petty things weren't so petty after all because they were pieces of her, still, no matter how small. Pieces she never so casually gave away.

"Shouldn't that be better?" Elan looked up at her.

Caty shrugged. "I don't know."

He paused and gave her a puzzled look. "You'd rather have me as a stranger? The guy who only meets you for a couple of hours?"

"Well, clearly, this is exactly like that."

Elan argued, "We've had a day. We still have hours. Let's not—"

Caty interrupted, "And I like you."

She'd said this before, hadn't she? It was still true six months later.

"Everything you're saying should make this a good thing, but you're making it sound as if it's not."

She looked him in the eyes, pressing her lips together. He didn't say anything; just leaned back on the couch with a baffled look.

Caty realized he hadn't said how he felt about her when she had done just that. "Here's a question," she asked. "How were you expecting this night to end?"

His brows raised. "Honest?"

She nodded to encourage him.

Elan cleared his throat as he straightened his back and leaned forward. He stared away from her for a moment, then admitted, "Well, for one thing, you wouldn't be standing at the other end of the room."

Caty smiled, acknowledging that she had managed to put a space between them.

"And you wouldn't tell me you liked me as an excuse to avoid me."

She took a step closer to him as he continued.

"We'd sit on this couch and talk." He raised his hand and offered it to her. She took it, tentatively. "We always talk before one of us falls asleep. Shouldn't be any different now."

Caty put her foot up on the couch as she faced him, making herself a little more comfortable. "You never say good night."

"I don't?"

"Yeah, you just stop answering my messages."

Elan laughed. "That can't be true. I probably said it at least—"

"Nope," she shook her head. "It's okay. You just eventually reply to whatever I said last as if eight hours hadn't passed. No biggie."

"Now, you're lying," he argued, "I never get eight hours of sleep."

"I actually didn't count—I just assumed."

"Mmm," Elan nodded, "is this a passive-aggressive way of telling me that you don't like it when I don't say good night?"

"No, I'm just saying, you never do it."

"In the future, I'll say good night when I absolutely cannot open my eyes or move my thumbs anymore."

"You don't have to do it; your night is my day anyway."

"But you like it."

She looked down because she was embarrassed. "I do."

"Okay, then I'll start saying good night."

"What happens next? After the talk on the couch?"

She wanted to know if he had a plan, or at least an idea about how tonight would go.

"We go to bed," Elan shrugged, like she knew he would. "And maybe this time we don't sleep."

She took the throw pillow from behind her back and threw it at him. "Oh, what a line."

He caught the pillow before it hit his arm. "Well, it sounded different in my head."

Caty watched Elan laugh at himself. He was so open and inviting, unlike the first time they met.

"I don't know how to make it better," Elan admitted. "I like you. I wanted to see you. I came to New York for you. Was I hoping that something would happen? Sure."

Could she blame him? It's not like she hadn't thought about it too. The whole exchange over the past six months probably supported the assumption. It wasn't as if she hadn't flirted with him. She had. She liked him, plain and simple. She enjoyed his company, no matter how far or near he was.

Then again, he was leaving in a couple of hours. She didn't know how much time she had left now. She'd been counting wrong the whole time.

"I'm not saying that something should," Elan said quickly, raising his hands as if to surrender. "I'm not expecting anything. Seriously. I'm just happy to see you."

"I'm not being difficult," she whined a little.

"And I wasn't implying that you were easy," he answered.

Caty took a deep breath. A nagging thought in her head kept reminding her that she only had hours, and then all of this wouldn't matter, didn't mean anything in the long run. She pictured this night differently. She wanted to see him and have a good time, and then thought that they would part ways like they always had. Easy. Simple.

But maybe keeping in touch with him muddled their dynamic. She'd underestimated the situation; she can't possibly keep talking to someone through a gadget without getting tired of it.

And this really was long distance. They were half a day apart. And now that he was here, he was only gonna be for a day? She should just stick to her plan. "I'm seeing someone."

Elan straightened, as if something snapped. "You are?"

"Yeah, it's new. It's not like we're official yet, but you know. There's that."

He nodded, taking in this new information.

She did see a couple of men. She was new in New York. She was meeting new people every day. At the coffee shop, on her way to work, at her apartment building, at Riot! . . .

There's always someone.

"And before there wasn't anyone?" he asked.

"No one that mattered anyway."

Elan sighed. "So this one is special? That's what I'm hearing."

Caty answered, "I don't want to jinx it."

She didn't want to jinx anything. Hey, if she did meet a guy tomorrow after Elan left, she didn't want to risk it.

Elan raised his hands. "I didn't mean to."

"So yeah," she nodded. "It's not the main reason why we're not . . . you know. But I think we make good friends. I like talking to you. When I first met you, I thought you were kind of a bore, and you were off about me, I could tell." She unfolded her hands and shifted closer to Elan.

"I just wasn't used to you yet."

"Exactly. Now, you feel so familiar. In a weird way." She faced him and closed the distance they'd created. "I don't know. I'm only babbling because my thoughts are exactly like that. I have no idea what's going on. I thought seeing you would clarify things, but now I'm more confused."

"If you didn't want to see me, you could have just said so."

"But I do want to see you," she insisted. "I've been talking to you through a gadget for a good while, and sometimes it felt as if you weren't real. Sometimes I was convinced that I was talking to someone else. I can't seem to connect you from that night to the person I'm talking to now. You're hella entertaining."

"But not in person?"

"You are," she was quick to say. "Just, you know. I feel like I'm getting to know you in *that* space, and not in this one, the here and now." She gestured at him. "You just showed up looking like this, dropping details that I've mentioned, stuff I can't even remember . . ."

His hand reached out to her, and she grabbed it halfway. "Do you get what I'm saying? 'Cause I'm not sure I do."

"I think," Elan squinted, "you might just be overwhelmed?"

"How come you're not?"

"I am, are you kidding?" his eyes widened. "I'm in New York! For a day. Lucian is really good-looking. Ridiculously. And you live with him. How do you not fall in love with him?"

"Oh, I do! Every day." They laughed together, and he sort of sighed as he looked at their linked hands.

Elan dropped her hand and stood up. He walked to the window and stared at the lights of the city.

"I am happy to see you here." She rested her chin on the couch. "Even if I keep saying that it's weird."

"Thanks." Elan glanced back. "I am always happy to see you. Wherever. Whenever."

Then he walked over, took off his watch, and put it on the bedside table.

"Okay." He sat on the bed leaning on the headboard, both feet up. "So we won't do anything tonight."

"Okay?" Caty yawned. "I could leave and come back when it's time for you to go. Can we still grab breakfast before you fly out? This place has a really cool rooftop that we could check out. Do you have time for that?"

He tapped the space next to him. She gave him a look, but he insisted, "What? It'd be just like our first night."

"Well, we did something."

"No offense, but isn't it always something when it comes to us?" Elan pointed out.

No truer words had been said.

He looked so relaxed with his arm stretched out on the space he'd saved for her.

Elan scooted over as she rose from the couch, stopping at the edge of the bed.

"Did you ever do this with her?" Caty didn't know why she asked that, but it was a question she always had in mind.

"No," he answered right away, just when she thought she should probably be clear about whom she meant.

His hands reached up to hers, and their fingertips touched, ever so carefully.

"Are you still in love with her?"

"No."

Caty took her hand back and watched his fall back onto the bed. His brows furrowed.

"That's the first time you actually answered that question."

"I always answered the question."

"Yeah, but it always seemed as if you weren't really sure," she shrugged, imitating him.

"I don't shrug like that." He rose and knelt on the bed right in front of her.

She kept doing it, though, teasing him. So he wrapped his arms around her to stop her.

She wriggled out of his hold. "All right, I'll stop, I'll stop."

He leaned back, pulling her in, her knees touching the bed. Elan grinned like an idiot, and she suspected she looked the same too. Her eyes dropped to his chest as her hand touched him there. "What made you decide?"

"What? Knowing that I wasn't in love with her after all?"

She nodded, holding her breath. The entire time she had known Elan, she had believed he was devoted to Juliana, even though she was with someone else. He had been holding out for her, made a special trip to San Juan when she needed him.

"I think of myself as a patient man," he told her. Elan fell back on the bed, and she collapsed down with him, his arm finding its way around her waist. "I knew Jules had her issues. She was a mystery, so my way of letting her know I was there for her was to let her be, to make her feel in control. To make her feel safe."

Caty nodded, thinking how nice it would be to have someone who was patient and understanding. She wasn't the easiest person to love. She snapped a lot—liked to throw people off—and she could be loud and obnoxious at times. It was a defense mechanism, Otto once pointed out to her. She wanted to get rid of people before they could get rid of her.

He told her that was the reason they didn't work together. He told her she was acting like a child, and he was done with the games. She was too much.

"Then I remembered how it felt to want something so much I could barely contain it." His hand slid to her inner forearm, his fingers brushing her skin.

Caty gulped. His thumb started to stroke the skin just above her elbow. "And then?"

"I guess I'm more patient than I give myself credit for." He stopped stroking her to look her in the eyes. "I did just hear you talk about seeing somebody else after all."

Her breath caught in her throat, and her chest felt like a cage as her heart tried to leap out. Elan smiled at her, but it was full of a pain she wanted to wipe away.

He blinked and said, "But I had fun today. I like your routine."

He was changing the subject? After that, he was going to change the subject?

"I loved meeting your friends at Riot! Wish Jimmy was there, though."

She took a moment before making a sensible reply. "When I met Lucian, I was totally in love with him."

"How did you meet him anyway?"

"We liked the same boy. But I knew I'd lose out when I saw him."

"Whatever happened to the guy?"

Caty shrugged. "I don't really remember. I took Lucian instead. We were better off without him."

Elan's laughter boomed, and when it subsided, Caty muttered a curse to herself.

"What?"

"Nothing, I just—" Caty looked back at him. "I don't have anyone like you here."

He tucked a loose strand of hair behind her ear.

She bit her lip, recognizing the loneliness that had surrounded her since she moved to New York. Maybe since she'd first left San Juan. "Or anywhere in my life."

He paused, then said, "That sucks. I'd love to have someone like you and have her in the same country. Or in the same time zone, at least."

That idea pulled at her gut. She didn't like it at all. It felt as if she was being dumped out of bed and replaced by someone else.

She sniped, "You can't." Caty rested her chin on his chest. "I'm one of a kind, you know."

"Limited edition?" His fingers ran through her hair. He closed his eyes and groaned, "I've got an urge to tell you something, but it might ruin the moment."

"Mmm, I'm always interested in your urges," she grinned. "Is it dirty?"

Elan laughed, his fingers now massaging her scalp. She laid her head back down on his chest. "The internet sucks. Technology sucks."

"In the Philippines, I'm sure. But why?"

"Because I still can't touch you like this no matter how advanced they claim it is."

She wanted to throw out a funny remark, but what he'd said was so nice she wanted to linger in the moment. So she didn't say anything to ruin it.

Elan rested his arm on her shoulder. She lifted her head to check up on him. He was watching, and he caught her eye as she scooted closer.

They didn't say a thing, just smiled at each other and leaned in until their foreheads touched. He pulled away first and let his lips brush her temple.

He breathed her in, and she let go of her tension.

"Tell me again, why are we not doing this?" he whispered.

"Because I said so."

He agreed with a nod, but they didn't move away. They breathed in together, bracing themselves as they stood on the brink of temptation.

"Please stay," he said with a sigh.

Caty repeated what he'd said in her head. She closed her eyes and realized that it was exactly what she'd been afraid of hearing, not from his mouth but from hers.

eleven

"You do this thing, with your face," she told him, her finger tracing the bridge of his nose.

She always touched his nose before she kissed him, as if it was the most important thing on his face. Elan wasn't comfortable when people pointed out his crooked nose; it bothered him. But he let Caty do it. As long as she was near him, he was fine. He'd take what he could get, especially under today's circumstances.

He'd pictured it differently, hoping for a better turnout. He wanted this trip to New York to be a catalyst. They had been talking since she left after the Coronados' anniversary party, continuing what they'd started when they first met. But the last few months had been harder than the first ones. She'd moved to New York. She was adjusting. She had to repack, decorate her room, buy a rug, get a job, pick up a guy's dry cleaning, water his plants, order pizza or Chinese food, binge-watch *Seinfeld,* find a place with good coffee, mingle with people she met at parties in the hope of finding a better job, and decide which bagel shop had the best bagels.

Meanwhile, he had legal cases. He had started training for a marathon with his work friends. He'd adjusted to time differences. He brought laundry to Gia's place, checked on his niece, brought his mother to church and the clinic, visited San

Juan when he felt like it. And he waited. For her. For the time they were together on their screens.

Now he was here, and so was she.

Elan wiggled his nose. "I do not."

"I'm telling you as the person who gets to stare at your face while you nap."

"And I'm telling you, as the person who has it, I don't make that face." He leaned back. "And I didn't take a nap. I just closed my eyes."

Caty laughed. "You don't even know what I'm talking about."

"Do I even want to?"

She kept her hands on his jaw, her fingers rubbing his cheeks. "Maybe I'll just keep it to myself."

He paused to look at her, enjoying the sensation of her hands on his face. They'd been like this for half an hour, faces close and wrapped up in each other.

"I like you with this," she said, rubbing his stubble. She raised her hand and ran it through his hair. "And this."

"So I'm pretty much nailing it with hair."

"Makes you look more dangerous," Caty laughed again. "What do you like about me this time?"

"I feel like this is one of those trick questions." He smirked, his hand touching her arm. "I like you just the same. Is that an answer?"

"Sure."

He also liked the way she looked the last time—flowing red hair, gold dress, beautiful lips.

Elan ran his thumbs over her cheeks, smooth and pink. "Your hair looks good."

"You really have a thing for my hair, huh?"

"You change it every time I see you."

"Well, I only see you once a year. A girl has to get her hair cut. And dyed."

"Hey, it hasn't been a year since we last met."

"I change my hair a lot," Caty answered. "I get bored."

He brushed her hair from her face and tucked it behind her ear. She looked up at him expectantly, as if she wanted an answer that would give her something specific, tangible.

"You know what I like most?"

She lifted her brows. "Tell me."

His thumb touched her lips and paused on her cupid's bow. "I know this." He smoothed the line that formed between her brows. "This is familiar. I know you." It was almost a whisper, but they were so close he knew she had heard not only the words but also the misery in them.

Her hand reached up to his wrist, eyes boring into him.

"This feels like coming home." He didn't think about how to phrase it before he said it; he just let it roll off his tongue. If he thought about it anymore, one of them would hesitate, and they would lose the moment.

Now he knew that sometimes, life offered you a window to stumble through into something wonderful. All one had to do was be present enough to recognize the opportunity and be brave enough to jump into it.

He had missed a lot of windows because he'd hesitated. Sometimes hesitating is wise; it saves you from recklessness and trouble.

But some things are worth the trouble.

Elan didn't want to miss the window again.

Caty bowed her head, forehead hitting his shoulder. "There's irony in that."

His hand slid back down to her arms, thumb circling the skin, hoping it would soothe her.

She scooted closer, pausing before she asked, "You working out now, Judy?"

Elan laughed at the abrupt change of direction. "Training for a marathon."

"God, why?" Her groan was muffled.

"It's for a cause."

Caty threw her head back. "Of course it is. It's always for the greater good with you."

"It's proving to be a good cause for you too, isn't it?" He squeezed her.

"You're so full of it."

Elan loosened his hold.

"Thank you," she said, and it was soft and delicate.

"What, is this over?"

"No," she pulled him in, hands digging into his skin. "We've got time."

Did they? He wanted to check but didn't. He guessed they still had a few hours.

Elan lowered himself to rest his head on her shoulder. She adjusted, putting her chin on the top of his head.

"Hey, Judy."

"Hmm?"

"Did you lie to me, ever?"

He cleared his throat, not sure this was a good question considering the mood. "You're a master of changing topics."

"I majored in it," she joked, her fingers curling on top of his head.

Elan took a second, opened his mouth, then sighed.

"That's not a no."

He lifted himself up to face her, head tilted. "Well . . ."

She frowned. Elan let out a ragged breath. He knew this day would come. He would have to tell the story. The right one. Not the version he told everybody else. "I don't play basketball."

She snorted, "No offense, but I didn't believe you."

He smiled as she urged him to continue.

"It was a late night. I was coming home from a game. I really was playing basketball. Not greatly—just average. I had snuck out when I wasn't supposed to."

Now that he was actually saying it, he couldn't help but spit it out. It wasn't rehearsed. He hadn't played it back in his head. Everything was just flashing at him, bits and pieces, smells and sights.

"The house was dark. Everyone was asleep. Except there was a light in the dining room, and I heard a sound like a crack. I thought we were getting robbed."

He looked at Caty's face and could tell she was confused.

"It wasn't a robbery. I went to my mom's room to check on her."

He remembered this much: his mom was crying on the bed, curled up in a fetal position. It wasn't the first time he'd seen her that way, and he didn't know how to approach her. She knew he was there, but she didn't run to the bathroom to hide her face as she'd done before.

"I checked the dining room. My father was there, standing by the table."

It was one of those wooden tables with a glass top. His fist was on top of a huge crack right by the edge. It was a vivid memory, the whole thing. The yellow lights in the dining room. His father's shadow on the floor. He remembered pausing before approaching his father. He had to. He remembered being afraid, but he'd done it anyway.

His jaw tightened. "My father has a temper. He drinks a lot. We all know that's not a good combo."

"He was drunk?"

Elan nodded. He and his sister had been told not to go near him when he was drunk, because he hit people. It was the alcohol, they said. But when Elan was in his teens, he had punched a classmate for teasing him constantly. It was the temper, like his father's, he always believed. But he rarely touched alcohol, afraid of what it would do to him if her ever had a bit of his father in him.

"Did you do anything?"

"Not really. But it seemed as if I had walked into something, and he didn't like it, so . . ."

"What happened?" Caty goaded him, knowing he was omitting details, things he couldn't say out loud because it would be awful to hear and even worse to say.

"He'd broken the glass on the dining table. I guess they were fighting before I came in."

Her hand flew to her mouth. He looked away, took a breath to fill his lungs with fresh air. "So I said some things and ticked him off."

Elan tried to look back at her. She looked horrified, so he quickly said, "It's fine."

"It's not," she snapped. "It's not fine."

"He was drunk. His aim sucked. I hit the wall when I tried to avoid him. That's why I have this," Elan pointed to his nose. *Not entirely true.* His father had hit him in the face when he asked about his mother. Then he hit the wall.

Elan tried to hit his father too. But he was a kid, and he wasn't used to fighting. He avoided fighting, always hated it. That's why he liked the law. He thought there was a better way to deal with conflicts.

She paused, trying to hide her shock. "What happened in the morning?"

Elan shrugged. "He didn't remember all of it. So we just said it was because of basketball."

"And he believed you?" she exhaled. "Was that the only time?"

No. There were other times. Not just punches. "We had help from outside. That's where I met Pascual, you know?"

His uncle Pascual, the man he worked for now. They had asked for help, and he had given it to them pro bono. Since then, Elan had never left the man's side, even when Pascual insisted they didn't owe him anything.

Elan did owe him everything.

Pascual made sure their father could never come near them or hurt his mother again. So his father left them alone completely, as if it was a relief to finally be free of them. Elan hadn't seen the man since.

"Same guy you work for?"

Elan nodded.

"That's nice," she mused.

Elan looked directly at her. "You shouldn't feel bad for me. It was a long time ago."

"That doesn't make it right."

He lay on his back and stared at the ceiling. The truth slipped from his tongue. "Sometimes, I get scared that I've inherited his temper."

Caty paused. "You count to ten under your breath when you're getting mad."

He smiled. "You noticed."

"Someone taught me the same thing."

"It's become a habit," he admitted. "A precaution. I don't know. I don't want to risk it."

Caty rolled over to face him. "You think one day you'd just snap?"

His jaw twitched. "I think about it, yeah."

He didn't say anything then, just took a couple of deep breaths after realizing what he'd done. He'd told the story. He'd never told it to anyone before. The only people who knew were his mother, Gia, and a childhood friend.

And it wasn't so bad.

He was still breathing.

He was still . . .

Elan turned to Caty. "Does it scare you that I have that history?"

He meant that it ran in his blood—that he might have the tendency, the probability. But mostly he was ashamed that he had a father like that.

Caty pursed her lips. "Should it? Did you ever hit anyone before?"

"Kid from school."

"Why?"

Elan suddenly felt very awkward about the conversation. "Nothing. I was young. I got picked on; I fought back."

"Did you feel like you had to; it was necessary?"

"At the time? I don't know. I wasn't thinking." He knew he was giving her brief answers, but he didn't want to talk about it anymore. Maybe the discussion had gone further than what he was comfortable with.

"Hey," Caty's brows met. "You're the one who brought this up."

"Yeah, but . . ." he exhaled through his nose.

She lay back down and didn't speak for a moment. "Maybe it should scare me."

He lay completely still. That was one of his greatest fears, for someone to find out and use this truth against him. It's why he never got too involved in relationships, didn't explore further. He thought it would be better if he just stuck to the people who already knew about it or those who wouldn't force him into telling. Then there was also that paralyzing fear that he could just snap; he could hurt someone, like his father had.

Her hand grabbed his, making him snap back to the present. She spread her fingers across his hands, radiating heat to his cold palms. "But I'm more concerned about you; does that make sense?"

He was in New York, in bed, with her. Of course it made sense. Elan swallowed and blinked at the ceiling. Was he going to cry? He couldn't, *shouldn't*.

Her fingers interlaced with his. "As awful as that was, if it hadn't happened, I'm not sure I would have wanted to meet you."

He cleared his throat. "What do you mean?"

Caty lifted herself up over him and spread her legs on either side of him. His hands slid to her hips as she lowered her weight on top of him.

"It's my favorite thing about you."

Elan snorted. "My nose?"

She shushed him. "Shut up. Your nose was the first thing I noticed about you."

Confused, he let her talk.

"It's the main reason I kept bugging you that day in the car," she continued. "I wanted to know the story. Can you imagine what would have happened if you didn't have the most interesting nose?"

Elan shook his head. Caty smiled.

"Your hair," Elan spoke. "Not the first thing I noticed about you."

She looked puzzled. "It's not?"

Elan rolled her over to her back, staring at her face as he settled on top, careful not to crush her.

"What was it?"

His thumb brushed the bottom of her lip.

Eyebrows raised, she breathed, "*Oh*."

Her eyes sparkled, and the smile she rewarded him with was wide and giddy. Whatever wall had been between them collapsed. She was Caty, free and unfiltered. Like before.

She let the tip of her nose touch his. "Hey."

He closed his eyes.

"Thanks for telling me about that," her voice was calm, and he felt her hand touch his cheek. "It was really . . ."

"Shitty?"

"No," she smiled up at him. "Personal. I could tell you haven't talked about it with other people a lot."

"I never . . ."

"I'm glad you feel like you could entrust me with that," she said.

"Yes, well, you almost saw me naked the same day you met me, so I might as well share my deepest, darkest—"

Caty laughed, an unexpected outburst.

"And clearly, the memory of it brings you such joy."

She kissed him then, hand on his nape, pulling him down. He responded the way a man lost in a desert would upon seeing a stream of water. He caught her kiss and drowned in it.

And what a feeling that was, to finally drink from the cup and relieve his doubts. But he did remember that she had said no to this earlier. He came up for air, regretting the space between their lips, and said, "Wait."

She looked delirious—pink cheeks and swollen lips. "What?"

"That guy you said you were seeing—"

"Is not here," she finished, pulling him back in.

Elan kissed her, then insisted, "I don't want to get in the middle of things."

She held his face with both of her hands. "Elan. You're the mayor of the gray area. You have always been in the middle of things."

"But—"

"*Oh my god, this is like our first night.*" She let go of him, groaning in frustration.

"No, no," Elan said quickly, "I'm just making sure this is what you want."

A line formed on Caty's forehead, and the ends of her lips turned down.

"Tell me what you want." He lowered himself, catching her hand before it hit his chest. He wondered how much time they had left but realized that it wouldn't matter anyway. Elan knew he would never have enough time in the world to tire of her.

Caty's fingers unbuttoned his shirt, her eyes focused on his, letting him know she wanted this. So he kissed her again, as she demanded, with one hand grabbing her face. She opened her mouth, and his tongue curled against hers. A surge of electricity shot through him, alerting all of his senses.

Caty broke the kiss and leaned forward, pushing him down on his back. She smiled in that mischievous way of hers as she got on top.

He grabbed the hem of her shirt, but she voluntarily took it off in a slow, deliberate manner.

"You're killing me," he breathed out. "Right now. You're killing me."

"Already?" She tossed the shirt aside, but he didn't follow it. He was exploring every inch of her uncovered body with his eyes. With the lights on, her skin looked soft and smooth, and he couldn't help but wrap his arms around her waist.

Caty leaned in but didn't kiss him, not yet. "Listen."

Listen? More talking? His hands protested, running across her back, looking for that clasp. He felt her laugh, her lips grazing his cheek.

"Elan," she called him again. "I want you to be patient for a little while."

Her hands slowly traveled from his chest to his belly, then farther down, until she unbuttoned his pants.

"Please?" she asked, moving slowly away from his face, her hair leaving a trail. She kissed his neck, then his chest, all the way down to his stomach.

"Caty, I—"

She reached that part where he most felt the need. Caty paused, eyes looking up at him, hair falling on her face. Elan reached out, fingers running through her hair, and gripped, holding her hair back for her. Her face lit up.

With his back hunched, Elan watched as those lips—the very ones he couldn't tear his eyes away from on that first day—parted and kissed the rest of him.

How could he ever leave her now?

The last time they did this, it was a battle. Who would get there first. Tonight, it seemed like a contradictory display of control and submission.

Caty let him kiss and caress and knead parts of her that wanted to be touched and needed the attention. She was at the mercy of his mouth—teasing, licking, and tasting her, as if she were dripping honey.

For her part, she was pulling and grabbing hair, scratching and digging at his skin, arms tangled and legs quivering, close to the edge.

Elan came up to kiss her mouth as she felt his weight on top of her. She moaned, thought how much she loved this part most of all, sharing the warmth of another person, skin grazing skin, breaths colliding.

She braced herself for it, seeing him reach out to the bedside table, hearing the sound of foil ripping.

She squeezed her eyes shut, just waiting, dying, chest about to explode, when she heard him call her name.

She jolted, eyes opened to meet his. He didn't look as if he'd changed his mind, which was what she feared the most, remembering their last time. His eyes were calm, like a peaceful ocean at dawn. His brows furrowed ever so slightly, and his jaw tightened.

Then she felt him crash against her in a swift motion.

She gasped, arching her back as he dropped his head to her neck, pulling and pushing, bodies writhing to find a harmonious pace.

When he looked back at her, his eyes were darker, brows creased and forehead adorned with beads of sweat. His mouth was a thin line as he increased his pace, sending her stomach and legs quivering until she finally soared to the edge.

It was flying. No contraptions, her arms like wings, wind caressing her face, her hair wild and free. She felt herself open up as the adrenaline rushed to the tips and ends of her body.

Caty sensed Elan falling apart seconds later, and she watched him let out a groan as he reached his end.

She welcomed him back in her arms, like the sea to the shore, cradling him as their chests heaved, rising and falling at the same time.

She was speechless—breathless—until laughter bubbled up, surprising them both.

He turned to her, looking so concerned that it kept her laughing. She couldn't help it.

"What?" Elan asked, and she laughed even more, seeing that he was flushed, not just because of what they'd done but possibly from embarrassment.

"Nothing."

"You came, right?"

"Yes, yes," she smiled. "I came, I saw, I fucking conquered."

Elan chuckled under his breath.

Caty grabbed his cheeks with both of her hands. "You're the killer."

She saw a new glint in his eyes—a side of him she hadn't seen before, and she liked it very much. "Who knew, huh?"

He leaned forward to kiss her again—no, bite her lip—and by the looks of it, he did.

twelve

Caty's eyes opened, and it was like waking up to remembering something she'd forgotten. Locking the doors. Turning off the faucet. Closing the windows.

She lay on her side, afraid to look over and find the other side of the bed empty. He probably would've left by now.

When she turned, her heart sunk. The other side of the bed was smoothed out, a stark contrast to the way it had been last night. She was alone. She didn't get any pleasure from knowing she'd been right in the first place, knowing she'd wind up alone.

She heard a sound like water was running in the bathroom. *Did we leave the faucet on?* She sat up in bed, blinked, and kicked off the sheets. Then she found the shirt he'd been wearing last night lying on the floor, so she put it on to cover herself momentarily and headed to the bathroom. She peeked through the slightly open door and then simply pushed it back.

There was his back, and his face reflected in the mirror. His eyes widened when he spotted her, his hand still holding a toothbrush.

Elan was in the bathroom. Brushing his teeth.

He took his eyes off her to spit in the sink, gurgle, and wipe his face with a towel. His hair was wet, which meant he'd already taken a shower and he was getting ready to leave her.

She remained at the door, her hips leaning on the frame, watching him as he laid his palms on the sink. He looked at her through the mirror. "Hi. Good morning."

"I thought you'd left."

He bowed his head.

"Are you still leaving?" she asked. Something awful was growing in the pit of her stomach—butterflies: tiny, fluttering wisps of hope and expectation.

She took a step closer, then another. When she reached him, she saw that he was holding his breath, as if to stop himself from saying anything.

Caty's hand snaked around him, and she rested her head on his shoulder. She heard him exhale. Loud.

It can't be good.

Her fingers spread to his stomach and rested on his tensed muscles. She lifted her chin up to his shoulder and looked at their reflections in the mirror. She smiled at the image, both of them rumpled comfortably, like a couple who normally shared their space together.

Maybe if we lived in the same city. Maybe, she thought, then pulled away.

He laid his hand on top of hers and pulled her back in. "I'm sorry."

She pressed a kiss on his shoulder and stepped back. "I'll get dressed."

But he didn't let go of her hand. He pulled her in and lodged her between him and the sink. "I've had this shirt for a while, but it didn't look as good on me as it does on you."

She smiled and bowed her head a little bit, feeling her cheeks get warm. "I'd come closer if I didn't have morning breath."

He looked at her funny and lowered his head to peek at her face. He tipped her chin up and kissed her, quickly, the way couples do normally before rushing to work or leaving each other for five minutes.

"You're good," he confirmed.

She laughed, smacking her lips. "Minty."

"Hotel toothpaste." He leaned back and let her jump on the sink, even gave her a little boost so she could sit down. "I wasn't just gonna leave you."

She nodded. What else could she say? He caught her eye and smiled.

"You seriously thought I was gonna do that?"

"Well, I . . ." She'd done it to him the last time, hadn't she? She thought it would be easier to just get up and leave, to avoid the awkward goodbyes. This time wouldn't be too awkward, she imagined, but it would be *difficult*. The look he gave her convinced her that the more they stayed together, the harder it would be to part.

But she was going to take it as it was. She and Elan had been together for a day. She supposed she just had to make it count.

Elan could see that she was shutting down right before his eyes. She was hesitating, stopping herself from smiling—avoiding him again. He hated it, because he had less time to convince her to open up again, to be the girl he'd been with just a couple of hours ago, the girl who threw caution to the wind and believed in him, in *this*.

He leaned closer and rested his chin on her shoulder, staring at his reflection behind her in the mirror. He watched her head lean toward him and knew he had to keep trying.

Elan felt her arms snake around him. "Are you okay?"

"Yeah," she answered. "Can we stay like this a little longer?"

"Yeah. We have time."

She rested her head on his chest, breathing in and out before asking, "Do you need help packing?"

"I'm mostly okay." He didn't have a lot of stuff, just the clothes from last night, including the shirt she was wearing now, which he didn't mind.

Caty pulled away first and gazed up at him with a look he couldn't quite grab, but he thought it had a hint of resignation. "Oh, right. I should get out of this."

He tilted his head. "Or you can keep it."

She chuckled, pushing him a little to the side so she could get off the sink. "What, like something to remember you by?"

"No," he said immediately, frowning. *Something to remember him by?* Like it was a fucking souvenir, a nice memento from a vacation before they went back to real life. "Just something to keep."

Caty played with the hem of his shirt.

Real life. He couldn't help but think of it now, how it would all go back to what it was. Her, in New York. Him, in Manila. Her, seeing this man she told him about while he . . .

Elan bit his lip and shook his head slowly. That had bothered him last night, but he hadn't let it get to him. It was eating him up now.

"Or something to lose?" she said, heading back to bed. She pulled the shirt over her head without even bothering to unbutton it. She looked over her shoulder at him and threw the shirt back.

He caught the shirt by reflex and tossed it out of the way. "You have *all* the best ideas."

She giggled as he scooped her up and laid her back in bed. He crawled on top of her, kissed his way up, and stopped to look her in the eyes.

"Hi," Caty whispered.

Elan kissed her hello. It went on and on—the longest hello he'd ever said. He didn't want to stop, didn't want it to end, didn't want to kiss her goodbye. His ears were ringing as he kissed her senseless, and he could feel her pull him in closer with every start.

"Hey," she managed in between, "honey." *Not yet, not yet.* "Your phone." Elan sucked on her lip, and she leaned forward before grabbing his face. "I love what you're doing, but the ringing is driving me mad."

Ringing?

Then he heard the startling, loud rings in the background.

"It could be important," she added.

Elan leaped out of bed to find the phone and stop the annoying sound that filled the room. He grabbed the phone off the table, turned it off without even looking at it, and chucked it to the side.

He was back in bed in mere seconds, back to where he'd been.

"You know . . ." Caty started.

For a minute, he thought that maybe throwing his phone looked like a childish tantrum, but he didn't care. Couldn't care anymore. She had her legs wrapped around his hips, and *that* mattered.

"That whole temper thing could work for you."

His brows furrowed.

She nodded to the phone. "That was cute."

"Just cute?" Elan laid his palm on her lower belly and let his thumb graze down. Her hips buckled at the touch, and that gave him pleasure.

"That was hot." She unlocked her legs from his hips and spread them for him like an invitation, approval.

"How'd you like it this time?" he asked, lips grazing her hip bone.

"Slow." She wriggled in his hands, and her breath turned ragged. "Like we've got the whole day."

He saw the worry that skipped across her face, as if she regretted saying the words, but he kissed her before she could take it all back.

They never had enough time, but he would give this to her. Not as a parting gift but as a reason, a way, to convince her he was worth coming back to every time.

thirteen

They had some time.

Enough to say their goodbyes before the hotel doorman hailed a cab to take Elan to JFK. He kissed the top of her head while she wrapped her arms around him for the last time.

They had time. Not enough, never enough, but enough to matter.

They always had that.

Caty was on her way back home to her brownstone apartment in Bed-Stuy when she suddenly regretted not inviting Elan over so he could see where she actually lived, what it meant when she talked about the scenes she saw at her window.

At the front steps, she saw Lucian with his boyfriend, Jimmy, and friend Val. Lucian was statuesque—towering at six feet three with golden-blond hair. Jimmy was shorter and rounder, absolutely warm and lovable looking.

Lucian hooted at the sight of her. "Walk of shame, walk of shame!"

She laughed and answered, "Hey."

"Hey yourself," Val said. Val was younger than she was, a skinny boy who transformed into a Vivien Leigh replica at night. "Where's your lover from last night?"

Caty smirked. "I don't know what you're talking about."

Val rolled his eyes. "Sure. Hey, is that a hickey?"

Caty lifted her shirt to cover her collarbone, then turned to Lucian. "How was last night? Sorry, I didn't get to say goodbye."

"Splendid," Lucian answered. "We're on our way up to the apartment—Val was just leaving."

Val agreed and air-kissed everyone before heading out.

Caty's shoulders sagged when Jimmy put an arm around her. "How you doin', love?"

They climbed up to their unit. Jimmy was the cook in the household, so he went straight to the kitchen to make breakfast for all.

Lucian sat at one end of the couch while Caty took the other. "How was last night?"

Last night—the words made her want to lie down on the floor and weep.

"Oh, *babe.*" Lucian clicked his tongue and pulled her in, aware that she seemed about to slide down the couch and drop on the floor. "I can't tell if you had the best or the worst night."

She couldn't decide either. She was convinced that it should be the former, but she was feeling the latter.

"Did you get to talk about your . . . arrangement?"

"Yes, but we got distracted."

Lucian arched his eyebrows. "So you had a splendid night indeed."

"I told him I was seeing someone."

"Are you? That grimy boy from the hipster coffee shop?"

"No," she cried. "God, not him. But there's always someone to see."

"*Ah,*" Lucian nodded. Caty knew he had something on his mind, but he was holding back. "And what did he say about you seeing someone else?"

She shrugged. "Does it matter? We slept together anyway."

"He didn't say anything?"

"He said," Caty heaved a sigh, "that he's patient."

Lucian snorted, pulling back to look at her face to check if she was serious. "Yeah? But is that enough?"

She scratched her cheek.

"Let me tell you one thing," Lucian paused. He took a moment before saying, "I'm no expert . . ."

But Lucian had Jimmy, and that was success in Caty's book. Jimmy was wonderful—loving and accepting, committed to Lucian, and he made the best cinnamon French toast.

"I've always thought that for a relationship to begin, one person had to be braver than the other."

"Just one?"

Lucian nodded. "Someone has to dive in first. It's never the two of you, together. It's nice to think of it that way, but there's always someone who lays out all the cards first."

"Was it you or Jimmy?"

"It was him, of course." Lucian laughed.

Caty laughed with him, rubbing her eyes because she'd had so little sleep. She knew she wouldn't be sleeping much anytime soon, though.

"No one wants to go first," Lucian added.

"That's because only stupid people do that," she spat. Yes, she never had trouble making the first move, but this already felt too big to just go ahead and jump in. This was a high dive. "Smart people assess risks."

"Again, like I said, one has to be braver than the other."

They stared at each other, not saying a word.

"You think it should be me?"

"I didn't say that."

"It should be him." Caty frowned.

"Why?"

"Because," was all she could think of.

"I don't get why you're hesitant about this. You don't have a problem letting men know you want them."

"I don't," she agreed. "He knows that."

Lucian cocked an eyebrow to tease her.

Caty shook her head then covered her face with her hands.

"What's wrong?" Lucian asked.

"Nothing," she answered too quickly. "I already told him I was seeing someone."

"So? Tell him you changed your mind."

"I can't just change my mind," she reasoned. "This guy was supposed to be special."

"But you only made him up."

"Lucian."

"Catalina," Lucian sighed with exasperation.

"I can't do it," Caty whined. "I can't go back to texting and calling. I'm not gonna do the long-distance thing."

"What is so bad with long distance? I did it."

She smirked, "Yes, and as I recall, you complained about it constantly. You threatened to break up with Jimmy five hundred times before getting here."

"Okay, fine. But even after last night? His love bites didn't help?"

"*Especially* after last night."

Lucian paused, thought about it, then nodded ruefully. Jimmy came back to the living room with a ladle in hand.

"Should we use the table like normal adults or eat on the couch?"

"Couch!" they both answered.

Jimmy smiled and walked back to the kitchen.

"You don't have to text him; *sext* him," Lucian grinned.

Caty threw a pillow at him.

"You know what else I think?" Lucian stood, poised to remove the contents of the table in front of the couch. "The one who goes first is usually the one who wants it more."

Caty thought about that, watching him put away the magazines and the fake plant.

"He lives twelve hours ahead of me," was all she said.

"So you'll get valuable foresight."

"Lucian, please," she begged.

"Honey," Lucian faced her, hands on his hips, "you're thinking too far ahead. One foot after the other."

"Who's putting one foot after the other?" Jimmy asked, both hands holding plates with two pieces of his French toast, eggs, and bacon.

"Nothing," Caty answered, jumping to her feet to grab a plate.

He pulled it away before she could get it and scolded, "No breakfast until you tell."

"It's the nap guy."

"The nap guy," he repeated, because he knew about Elan, of course. Living with Lucian and Jimmy meant sharing French toast in the morning, going out at nights, watching reruns of old sitcoms, and telling each other everything.

"Lucian thinks I should give it a try."

Lucian took his plate. "I didn't say that. And even if I did, she's obviously talking herself out of it."

"Why?" Jimmy gave her the plate. "And judging from that love bite, I assume you've passed the napping stage?"

"Was it good?" Lucian interrupted.

Caty rolled her eyes. "What do you think? I have a hickey. It goes right down to here."

"The biting kind," Jimmy supplied, looking impressed.

Caty raised her voice a little to get them back on track. "He lives an ocean away from me."

"So have phone sex, for God's sake. You touch yourself—don't think we don't hear it," Jimmy observed, as if it was so obvious. "Here's to hoping he's as fluent as he is durable."

"That's it? That's the answer to this?"

"Well, you're not having sex with anyone here," Lucian mumbled, mouth stuffed with toast. "Except with yourself. He's right; these walls are too thin."

"What about me?" she retorted. "I hear you guys too!"

"More reason for you to have sex on the phone."

"It's not just about the sex. It's everything, okay? I can't have a relationship with a gadget."

"I hear they're developing stuff for that," Jimmy added. "Plus, you're not gonna be away from each other the whole time, right?"

"I don't know; he lives in Manila."

"But is that a permanent thing?" Jimmy asked.

Caty knew what he was implying, and that was the very thing that she was afraid of. She can't ask someone to change his whole life for something that even she wasn't sure of. Would it be worth it?

But Lucian wasn't done. "May I remind you of your meltdown after that one date?"

That date. The one where she just had to check her messages. It was a couple of weeks ago, while she was settling in and agreed to go out with a Riot! bartender named Jordan. He was hot, and he'd asked her out as soon as she took her perch on the barstool. They went as far as kissing, and when he invited her up to his flat, she only ended up running back down.

"Well, maybe I can get over it now."

"Because you broke up with the nap guy?" Jimmy asked.

"We didn't break up." Caty rolled her eyes.

"I think you broke up with him."

Caty wiped her face and wondered, "What?"

"You told him you were seeing someone," Lucian pointed out.

"I'm allowed to see someone. It's not like we said we weren't gonna do that."

"Is he seeing someone else?"

The thought made her frown. "No." She remembered how Elan looked when she told him she was seeing another guy. He was obviously surprised, and if it had been her on the other end, she would have looked far more shocked.

She felt guilty for that tiny lie, but then again, maybe it was the right thing to have said.

Lucian waved his hand. "Then by all means, go test your theory. But if you still can't sleep with someone else, then you need to call that boy."

Caty rolled her eyes. "And have phone sex?"

Lucian's lips spread into a smile. "Sure, if that's your prerogative. But I think it'd be nicer if you told him how you truly feel."

He didn't need this. Not after that grueling flight. Not after the delays and the crying baby in the background. Not after seeing Caty standing on the street as his cab pulled away.

He went straight to the hospital, where his mother was. He'd finally gotten a text from Gia explaining what had happened, saying at the end, *Don't worry, I got it under control.*

But Gia had a six-year-old who went to school every day, a husband who wouldn't be returning from his job away from home until the end of the year, and no extended family near enough to help her.

He had always been the one to take their mother to checkups, to church, to Sunday lunches with relatives or friends.

"What are you doing here? I said we're okay," Gia insisted. He wasn't expecting a welcome, but he certainly wasn't happy with what he got. After all the back and forth he went through about staying or leaving, he was welcomed back with this?

Elan narrowed his eyes. "Have you slept?"

"I'm fine. How was your trip?"

He shrugged. "It was okay. I'm here."

"Elan."

"Gia." He closed his eyes because she had that tone. He knew it so well, and he didn't want to argue. He wanted to believe that he'd done the right thing flying back early. Unfortunately, he'd been plagued with worry that he'd been wrong, and if he had discussed the decision with Caty before, he knew that she would have made a much more sensible point. But he was here now and he would deal with it.

"She's fine," Gia said. "She'll be discharged in the morning. I tried calling you, but you didn't pick up."

"Was already flying back."

"Did you get to see what you wanted to see?"

He avoided that and pulled up a chair next to his mother. "Yes, it was fine. Don't worry about it."

"Funny, I thought that's what I said," she quipped.

He breathed through his nose and didn't respond so that would just end the discussion. Elan wanted quiet, or at least a quiet place, even though his thoughts weren't allowing him to get a wink of sleep.

"Did you even stop by your place first?"

He snapped, his voice rising, "God, Gia. Can you drop it? I'm already here."

He saw her lean back and wince.

God damn it. He looked away, face twisted with irritation. *Calm down.* He started breathing slowly and counted to ten.

"It's okay," she said, her voice cutting through as he got to three. "Elan. Look at me. It's okay."

Four.

"Elan, you're not like him," she announced. "I know that. You know that. We all know that."

Five. Six. Seven. Eight. Nine. Ten.

He extended that last breath before turning back to her. Gia looked at him, then shook her head. They did this all the time, staring each other down until someone gave in first.

They'd fought over chores when they were kids, but after their father left, they stopped arguing about petty things like taking out the garbage or cleaning the windows.

A loud ring cut through the room and broke the staring contest. They looked around for the source of the sound.

"Your bag," she said.

He opened the zipper, grabbed his phone, and read the name on the screen: *Caty.*

"Take it," Gia ordered.

He wasn't planning to drop the call, so he left the room to do it. He cleared his throat to shake off the negativity hanging around him.

Elan answered, mustering all the strength he had not to sound pissed off or upset. "Hi."

"Hey?" Hesitation.

He cleared his throat again and decided to try and do better. The fact remained that he and Caty were right back where they had been before the trip. He couldn't see her—or even worse, touch her—when he wanted to.

"Hey. Everything okay?" he asked.

"Yeah." She sighed, hesitation still lingering in her voice. "Just checking to see if you made it back in one piece."

"Oh."

"Are you? In one piece?"

Elan looked down, as if he really needed to check. "I think so?"

"Good," she said, then muttered, *Good, good.*

A thick silence followed, pure radio silence. He couldn't say anything else. His mind was frozen as he stood there in the hospital lobby. If she asked, he couldn't lie about where he was, as he'd done before when his mother had been in the hospital.

"It's just that," Caty started again, "my week's pretty slammed. Hans is hosting a party for all of these important people."

She went on about it, but somehow all he could think was that she was seeing someone. *In New York*. Where he was not. Annoyance and disappointment overwhelmed him.

"So I might miss the premiere on Friday," she explained, talking about that show they agreed to watch together.

"And you're seeing that other guy, right?"

There was a pause. "What?"

"You're going to keep seeing that guy while you conveniently have me in this weird virtual space—" he blurted.

"*Hey,*" Caty snapped. "You're kidding, right? Nothing about you is convenient."

He knew he should dial it back. He knew that. He was picking a fight at the worst possible time, but he'd been in a really bad funk since riding the cab to JFK. It had just been a too-long bad day. "I get it. We live in different places."

"It's not just that," she reasoned. "You're half a day ahead of me."

"Yeah, but I never ask you to stay up for me."

He heard her sigh, "God, that's not it either."

"Then what is it?"

"Why are you bringing this up now?"

She was right; of course, she was right. They should have talked about this when he was right next to her, and he could tell her, *Please, stop seeing other people. Let's give this a real, proper try.* But they hadn't, and that was killing him.

"I'm just so sick of staring at my phone," Caty said. "Every time you go to sleep, I can do anything I want, but I just end up waiting for you to wake up. What is *that?* I don't want to keep doing it."

Elan blinked a few times, and his back slouched.

"I need a break," Caty continued. "I just moved to New York. I want to be present here, but I feel as if I'm in this bubble with you. And you have needs."

"Don't talk to me about my fucking needs," he complained.

"Fine. Then *I* have needs," Caty insisted.

"Weren't they met just a few hours ago?" he blurted out. "Or was that too long ago for you?"

Elan heard her gasp. He really should just end the call. Drop his phone. Throw it at a wall. He hated how he sounded and how that must have hit her.

It took awhile for her to speak. "Look, this was never supposed to be—I don't know how to do this." She recovered. "We weren't supposed to keep talking."

"You could have just said. I didn't know I was wasting so much of your time."

"That's not what I meant," she was quick to say.

"Then tell me, Catalina, whatever did you mean by that?" He knew he sounded harsh, but he wanted the answers. If she thought that they weren't supposed to keep talking, then everything that had happened in the past few months seemed like a lie. Even that night. *Especially that.*

It was so quiet on the other end that he thought for a minute that she was no longer there.

"Why can't you come home?" he mumbled.

"What are you talking about? This is my home. I am home. My life is in New York," she blurted out. "This is exactly my point."

"I can't be in New York," he responded, looking around the bare walls of the hospital. He was frankly getting sick of its smell and how it was so bright yet dark at the same time. "I'm needed here."

He heard her sigh. "Elan. Nobody asked you."

Elan took a deep breath. Frustration and regret had swirled around him the whole day, but this felt like a sudden stop. His hand became limp as he set the phone down and ended the call. He walked as fast as his feet could take him out of the hospital and into the parking lot. There was a heaviness in his chest, and it felt like there was a plastic bag over his head. He couldn't breathe, but he kept walking until he found a corner.

He opened his mouth to catch his breath, but he let out a scream that echoed throughout the lot. The release made his knees buckle, so he crouched for a minute, put his head between his knees, and breathed slowly.

He told himself in between breaths that there would be tomorrow, and by then he would be better at this. Maybe he wouldn't be so upset. He wouldn't be so emotional, and he would find a sensible voice.

He had to believe all of that would be possible.

PART

Four

The more you love someone, he came to think,
the harder it is to tell them. It surprised him that strangers
didn't stop each other on the street to say I love you.

JONATHAN SAFRAN FOER

fourteen

ONE MONTH LATER

Caty went back to Riot! that night to watch Lux do her first Mariah Carey impression. She wanted to be current, but really, Lux killed "Touch My Body" all the time.

She sat on a stool by the bar and greeted a few friends. Jimmy was supposed to be there, and she guessed he'd arrive soon. He was never late for Lux's performances. He was always there for her now that they no longer had to cross borders to be together.

"What can I get you?"

Caty turned to find Jordan leaning on the bar in front of her. "My usual. I'm shocked you haven't prepared it yet."

He grinned, reached down, and grabbed two shot glasses. "I need an extra second to have you stare at my face."

She smiled and watched him pour the tequila. He set the glasses down on the counter. One for her, another for him.

They clinked glasses, smiled at each other, and drank. It burned its way down her throat, all the way to her stomach.

"How's Lux doing?" she asked, her voice loud so Jordan could hear her.

"Two shots before going back."

"Really?"

"She looked banging, though," he added, his smile lighting up the bar. He was so pretty she almost regretted running out of his apartment on their first date.

But then again, she didn't. That horrible feeling in her stomach threatened to return, so she tapped her glass on the counter.

Jordan raised an eyebrow. "That kind of night?"

He was sweet, in spite of the amount of ink on his arms that made him look tough.

"How was the shoot today?" he asked.

Caty's shoulders slumped. "Okay, I guess."

"Relax, babe, you're good. I saw what you did to our apartment."

"That was cleaning out your space, not styling."

They were better as friends anyway. She'd realized that as the weeks went by, in spite of her attraction to him. When Jordan inherited a bunch of furniture from his grandmother, Lucian asked Caty to assess which pieces were good enough to keep and which were better off sold or auctioned. So she rearranged the furniture and convinced Jordan and his roommate to sell some leftover pieces on the internet or at the flea market.

She'd made some money on the job, and it was a nice change from being someone's assistant. That had gotten old so fast.

Jordan refilled her glass and looked sternly at her. "I'm keeping tabs."

"I'm sure," she answered, taking the glass off the counter and downing it in one go. She grimaced.

"Come over tonight; we're having an after-party. We can talk about your shoot."

Your shoot. He said it like, *your* shoot, as if it was the biggest of all deals. Well, she supposed it was. One of her former clients from Toronto had called and wondered if Caty could shoot something for her website.

When she got the call, it felt like rain after a drought. So she really wanted to ace it. It was real work, not watering plants, picking up laundry, or walking a dog named Mando. Yes, she had actually moved up to walking her boss's dog.

But the shoot she'd done today? That was the kind of work she wanted. Work she knew and loved doing.

"Rain check?"

"Really?" he frowned.

"I'll tell you all about it when it goes well." Caty crossed her fingers.

Jordan clicked his tongue. "I'm telling you, babe. It will be great."

She leaned on the counter and gave him a sheepish smile. Really, Jordan should get a ribbon for giving her too many chances. He'd asked her out again, and she'd told him she was just trying to focus on her new life in New York, taking the next step for her career, and, hopefully, finding more friends. So here they were, friends supporting their other friend who was about to perform tonight.

"You get a free drink of your choice from your kind gentleman friend." He winked at her. Okay, so maybe they were friends— friends who still flirted. She'd be lying if she didn't admit that she loved the attention he gave. All the girls at the bar were basically swooning for Jordan. Someone please give the guy a medal for his face already.

"You're my favorite bartender," she shot back.

"Hey, Jordan, you're *my* favorite bartender," someone else yelled to get his attention.

Caty laughed.

The lights dimmed, and she turned around to face the stage. She always loved watching Lux perform. She was so beautiful and captivating onstage that even when they were young, Caty knew she was a star. Everyone who got to see her, even for the first time, thought so too. She was really proud of her friend following her dreams in this city.

Within that second, as much as her heart swelled with pride for Lux, she also felt it sink into her stomach. So she let the glass hit her lips, tipped her head back, and drank the dread away.

There was a knock on his door. That was strange, but it was even stranger that it was Gia on his doorstep.

"You gonna let me in?" She held a paper bag from a fast-food chain.

"I have to leave in an hour."

"I know," she agreed. "Sundays with Mom."

Elan nodded. They hadn't spoken much these past few days. He had started cycling seriously after the charity marathon the previous month and was spending Saturdays finding new routes. His phone was in silent mode on the counter, where it had been most days.

"Okay, you get dibs: thigh or wing?"

He frowned. "Thigh. Have you forgotten?"

Gia smiled. "I just wanted to get you to say something."

She handed him the food pack and took a seat at his tiny dining table. It wasn't a real dining table—it was more of study table with two chairs. He never used it anyway, since he wasn't in his apartment much.

"You haven't been doing your laundry," she said, looking a little cautious. He'd had his own washer and dryer for a while now, so he didn't do laundry at Gia's house.

"Yes, I have."

She leaned forward and sniffed him.

He batted her away with his hand. "Quit it. Why are you checking up on me?"

"Well," Gia grinned, "I haven't seen you in a while—"

"Busy."

Gia paused, chewing her food slowly.

He knew he'd rarely used that word with her, and her look said she didn't believe him. Could he blame her? In her eyes, he had always been a *yes* guy, to a fault.

She leaned back in her seat and took another bite. He braced himself for whatever she was going to say. Gia's visits were rare occurrences, so he knew this had to be big.

"Abby misses you."

He frowned. That was one of the things he missed about doing laundry at Gia's—seeing his niece, Abby. "Sorry. I'll drop by this week."

She nodded, took a moment before saying, "Is everything okay with you?"

Elan gave her a look, but she wouldn't budge. This was Gia. "I'm fine."

"I know you're fine. You've always been just fine," she grumbled.

Then what was this all about? He wondered.

"Are you angry at me for calling so much about Mom?"

He leaned back, let go of the spoon, and stared at her. "What? No."

"I thought you were."

"I'm not angry."

"Sorry, I know you hate the word *angry*. Were you annoyed?" she corrected herself.

Elan huffed, "I'm not anything, okay? I got a washer and dryer like you told me to, that's all. Pascual's been away so there's more pressure on me."

.

Gia gave him a smile, but it was thin. "You aren't always fine, you know."

What? He gave her a look. He had always been fine. He had to be fine.

"In fact, you were great until you got back from New York, and it was a good look for you." Her voice was chirpy, despite his mood. "It was a great look on you."

Elan rolled his eyes.

"Don't think I didn't notice," Gia continued. "You and your phone were inseparable. You smiled even when you were alone. You laughed . . ."

"All right," he cut her off. "You make it sound like something's wrong with me."

She raised an eyebrow. "No, nothing's wrong. You're just in love. And it's like you've never been."

Elan's mouth quirked. He knew that was true, but he didn't know how to handle it yet. He thought he would know when he saw Caty, but it wasn't as easy as he thought it would be. He didn't know what to do with himself and his affections. Then she told him she was seeing somebody else.

And why shouldn't she? She was a smart, attractive woman. Only an idiot wouldn't want to be with her.

Gia waited for his response but got too impatient. "If I ruined your trip, I'm sorry. I didn't think you'd rush home. I was only calling to let you know it was okay so you wouldn't worry too much. And I thought you finally had someone you couldn't just leave."

He blinked and held up his hand to stop her. "Okay, you're right."

Gia seemed confused. "About what?"

Elan took a deep breath and released it. The truth is, he just said it to tell her, *Enough. Stop.*

"How is she?"

If she meant the girl he did leave, then he wouldn't know. It didn't take long for their conversations to fizzle out. At first, one person didn't respond to the other for hours. Then it turned into days. Then . . . *nothing*.

That's just what happens. She'd found someone else. It happened so fast, yet watching and experiencing it had been so torturously slow. He'd lost.

His shoulders rose into a shrug.

"Oh no." Gia's face fell.

Elan smirked. "Don't worry about it, okay? I've just been a bit preoccupied these days. I'll come visit this weekend."

"But you have a washer here."

"I don't really go to your house just to do my laundry, you know. I go to get a free meal too."

She punched his arm playfully, and he made it look as if it hurt him more than she intended.

Even after he'd made her laugh, he felt her looking at him with sadness.

"So, does Mom have any activities today?" Gia asked.

Elan looked up. The change in topic made him think he might be safe from more questions. "Mass. Lunch. That's pretty much it."

"Sometimes I feel guilty because I don't get to do much for her," Gia admitted.

"You've got your hands full, with Abby."

"But that's it. We all have our hands full. We're all doing something. Even you."

He paused. "It's fine."

Gia snorted. "Did I just realize how many times you tell us you're fine?"

Elan was about to say, *But I am fine,* but he knew that wouldn't help his case.

"Elan." She looked him in the eyes, holding him in place. "You don't have to believe that you must take care of us. It's not your only job."

He blinked.

"I think—" Gia hesitated, meeting his eyes slowly before continuing, "even if it was the right thing to do, you still felt bad for what happened with Dad."

Elan looked away, shook his head. *Here we go.*

"You did the right thing."

"I know."

"But you lost a father." She reached for his hand, but he pulled it back. "I think you still blame yourself for that."

Did he? He wanted to say no, but his mouth felt dry.

"Don't punish yourself by thinking that everything that happens to us—the sole responsibility for taking care of us—is on you," Gia insisted, holding his hand again with both of hers. "You did that when you looked for help after that night. You saved Mom from years of abuse. You did it for me and for you too."

Underneath hers, his hand was balled into a fist. He swallowed but didn't look at her.

"Elan."

He shook his head. "I can't believe you're giving me this talk."

"I'm not giving you *a* talk," Gia pointed out, but her voice was soft. "I am talking to you. Someone should have done it a long time ago. It's way overdue."

"Exactly." He finally made the mistake of looking her in the eyes and recognized the tears welling up there. His hand softened.

"I just think that after what happened, when he left, we all assumed that we were fine," Gia continued. "Even if we weren't. It was a triumph but still a loss."

Elan licked his lips and gave her a quick nod.

"You don't have to be fine all the time." She smiled again, this time not out of pity but of kindness. "Especially when you're not."

He opened his mouth to say something, but he was at a loss for words. His tongue seemed to be stuck, so he swallowed to get rid of the lump in his throat.

"You only have a handful of people in your life," she stated. "You're as devoted to them as you are to us. It's why I thought—"

"It was a work trip, G," Elan replied.

"What happened to the girl?"

"I don't know." That was the easiest answer.

"How come?"

"I just don't know," Elan said earnestly. He really, truly did not know. She pulled the rug out from under his feet, and he had been agonizing about what he could have done differently. But he wasn't there, physically. He tried to bridge that gap with what he had, but man, proximity was everything. Long distance was just too . . . inconvenient.

"It's nothing," he concluded. He wanted to bite off his tongue after that. It tasted funny, most definitely bitter.

Gia's eyes narrowed. "It's not nothing. You look like you've been run over by a truck. Twice."

He pulled his hand away from her grip with a smirk. "Thanks, but it's just my face."

She scoffed, amused by his humor but clearly not done with the conversation.

"Look," Gia started again. "She lives far away, right?"

He was silent, neither confirming nor denying that fact.

"You only communicate through that." She pointed at his phone.

Again, he didn't even nod or shake his head.

"Do you think that's enough?"

He wanted to say it was, but he knew that wasn't true. It was never enough.

"You look like you're saying no," Gia said cautiously, happy to get a response from him.

Elan turned to her, now curious about where she was heading with this. But she stared right back at him with a look on her face.

"So?" he finally asked.

"So do something about it," she said, gazing at him intently.

As if he hadn't told himself that long ago. He scrunched up his nose in annoyance. "I can't move continents, you know."

"Of course not, dummy. It'll take years, and she doesn't have all that time to wait for you."

She was right. He knew Caty didn't have time to pine for him. She deserved more. Then what should he do? "I can't move to New York."

"Why not?"

Elan's eyes widened. "Because? Because it would cost a lot. Because I have a job. Because my family is here. There are too many reasons."

"There will always be reasons."

"But it would take years. I'd be uprooting myself. It would affect everything." He meant everything in the life he had now. He looked around his apartment and noticed the blankness of it.

Gia paused, lips spreading to a smile. "But you don't have to do anything if you don't want to."

He was annoyed at how smug she looked, like she knew it all. Elan clenched his hands into fists and growled, "But she's already over this whole thing."

Gia's smile faded, replaced with a look of alarm, concern. "She said that?"

"Yeah, she's seeing somebody else."

"Oh," Gia sat back in the chair and sighed. "Who?"

"I don't know," Elan's voice sank.

"Well, okay. Wow. I thought you guys really had something."

He shook his head. He'd thought so too, but clearly they were not on the same page. Maybe he was too late, despite the incredible night they'd spent together.

"Did she tell you why?"

He gave her a look. It was exhausting, trying to answer her questions—the same ones he'd been trying to answer on his own.

"We're apart," was the only thing he could say.

"Can you, for one second, remember what she told you? I know you would rather not think about it, but could you maybe review it?"

"Why?"

"Because when you're hurt or mad, you don't listen as well as you do when you're not. Maybe she was trying to tell you something."

"Yes," he answered straight. "She told me she was already seeing somebody else. I wasn't mad."

"But you're allowed to be. That's a valid emotion, you know."

Elan paused. The words hit him like huge blocks falling on his head. *You're allowed to be. That's a valid emotion.*

He didn't make any reply. He looked at his food and decided he didn't want it anymore. "We were just talking; nobody said anything about not seeing other people."

Gia nodded. It was quiet for minute, and he really thought it was over, that she was done asking about Caty, but Gia would always be Gia.

"But you've told her how you feel? She knows?"

Of course she knew. Didn't he show her how much? Didn't he tell her?

"Oh my God." Gia clapped her hands. "You didn't."

"I did too."

"Are you sure? She knew why you really came? You didn't even consider going on that trip before."

Elan tilted his head. "She knew that I wanted to see her."

"And?"

"She doesn't owe me anything," Elan answered.

Gia paused, then sighed and looked defeated. It was his turn to pat his sister's shoulders.

"Don't feel bad for me," he coaxed.

"I really wanted you to have someone. I'd like to know what she saw in that other guy."

"She probably sees him, literally, any time, any day. He's right there. I can tell you that much," he said dejectedly. "I have to go."

"One of these days," Gia sighed, "she's gonna realize that people don't just 'connect' so easily. You can't replicate that, you know."

He gave her a quick nod and licked his lips.

"Let's hope it's not too late."

Mariah Carey was a success. Caty listened to "Dreamlover" playing in their living room, watching Jimmy and Lucian dance and sing along. She was slouched on the couch, spacey from comfort and tequila.

She watched them kiss, and it made her laugh.

Jimmy turned to her. "Hey, smiley. What are you laughing at?"

Caty wanted to stop, but she didn't. She loved the sound of it, and it made her chest feel light to keep laughing, so she did.

Lucian reached for her arm to pull her up. "Come dance with us."

"I can't." She shook her head. "I'm glued to the couch."

He let go. "You're gonna make us carry you back to your bed, aren't you?"

"No, keep dancing," she said, waving her hand. "I'll watch."

Jimmy smirked. "I'll make you some coffee."

He disappeared into the kitchen, his favorite place. Lucian went ahead and sat next to her on the couch.

"You seem happy," Lucian started.

"I do?" Caty asked, looking at him with her eyes half closed.

"What'd you drink? You're all bubbly."

She shrugged. "Jordan juice."

"Are we finally tapping that?"

Caty laughed some more at what Lucian was insinuating. Really, laughing was fun, and she wanted to keep doing it. "No."

"Why not? He's all flirty when you're around."

"Just because," she asserted. *I don't want to,* her mind answered but never said out loud. The more she thought about it, the more she understood how simple it was. She was not with anyone here in New York because she did not want to be.

"Are you really okay?" Lucian asked, pulling Caty out of her thoughts. "Do you want to talk about it?"

"What makes you think I'm not?"

His eyes widened, as if it was so obvious and she couldn't deny it.

A shrill sound made them both jump. It was a phone ringing, and Lucian stood quickly to check his.

"Not mine," he announced. Jimmy called, "Not mine!" as well.

Caty nodded but stayed on the couch.

"Are you going to answer your phone?"

She frowned. There was no way she was in the right mind-set to answer a call. It was either her mother or her boss, Hans, who sometimes called her on Friday nights or weekends because he needed his assistant even on her time off. Lately, though, the calls were only from her boss. Her mother had fully adapted to texting instead of calling, so she rarely called.

"I'm on sabbatical."

"Since when?"

"Since today!" she exclaimed, and started thinking about how her boss would react to that. The ringing stopped, and it was quiet again, except for Mariah belting it out.

Jimmy came back to the living room with a mug.

Caty simpered, "You guys take such good care of me."

Lucian laughed. "Oh no."

"I'm not kidding," she insisted. "I'm so happy we all live together. Let's live together always."

Jimmy pulled her up to a sitting position and handed her the mug. "Sure. Let's live together always."

Caty blew on the coffee just as the phone started ringing again.

Lucian frowned. "All right, I'll answer it. This is just going to drive me nuts."

Caty's brows furrowed. "Could be Mom."

He shook his head, walking over to Caty's room. "She would have called me by now."

Caty agreed. It wasn't the first time her mother had checked up on her through Lucian.

"Where do you keep it?" Lucian shouted.

The thing was that since her last call with Elan, Caty had stopped using her phone completely. She rarely carried it, even at work, which ticked off Hans. Lately, she seemed to be doing a lot of things that annoyed him. Forgetting to switch to soy milk for his morning coffee was an even bigger mistake, especially since Hans was lactose intolerant.

Caty dragged herself out of the couch, walked to her room, and went straight to the drawer where she hid the phone. Right on cue, it started ringing again. She reached down through the balls of socks and grabbed it.

The screen showed an unknown number, so she wasn't sure if she should answer. But it was from a familiar country code that made her think about the worst possibilities—emergencies, accidents—so she did.

"Hello?"

"There you are!"

She recognized her brother's voice. "Whose number is this?"

"I changed my number. You should have known that, 'cause I texted you about twenty times already, but looks like you're not talking to anyone."

Her head tilted. "What happened?"

"No, what happened to *you*," Kip insisted.

"Nothing," Caty stretched her legs, relaxing. It had been awhile since she had talked to her brother, and right this very second she realized how much she missed him. "I'm unplugging. How are you guys?"

"We're fine."

"And the town?" She heard him hesitate. *Weird.* "Anything going on there? A dog baptism?"

"Not quite," Kip answered.

"Just say it."

"Not sure how you'll feel about it."

"One way to find out," Caty yawned.

"It's . . . Sarge," he said, his voice softer.

"Oh." She straightened her back. If it was Sarge, then it should be good. "What did he do this time? Open an acting school? Fund the production of a poorly cast play?"

"Well," Kip didn't sound amused. "He died."

Caty jolted. "Oh. No."

She wasn't a fan of Sarge, and she thought that most of the town wasn't too fond of him either. But what would San Juan be without him? Sarge, who always found a way to make parties bigger than they were.

"Yeah, it was sudden," Kip continued, explaining that Sarge had suffered a fatal heart attack at home. He was old, but he always seemed healthy. He lived for the town gossip—and Caty thought that was his secret for keeping fit and staying young.

Caty listened, the words jumbling in her head. She covered her face with her hand and actually, really, felt the loss.

"So we're having a big funeral next weekend," she heard Kip say. "We'll take out his yacht and spread his ashes over the sea."

"Whose idea was that?" she asked, even though she already knew. Sarge, of course it was Sarge.

"Casa Isabella is booked after. They'll be showing Sarge's movies and serving his favorites."

Caty smiled and felt a pinch in her heart as she imagined how it would all go. San Juan deals with funerals quietly, but this was Sarge Reynoso. "Okay, I'll be there."

"You what?"

She didn't know exactly why either, but she knew then that she wanted to see her mother, maybe tell her about the string of bad days that she'd been having. She wanted to hang out with her brother, watch a movie or go for a drive. The more she thought about it, the more she felt decided.

"I'll book my flight, and I'll be there."

fifteen

What's the protocol when a person you didn't particularly like—and everyone knows it—dies? Nobody invited her to Sarge's funeral. Although Caty assumed that everyone in town would show up anyway, she felt as if people were wondering why she was there.

She had just arrived from New York the night before, and now she was about to go out on one of Sarge's yachts with her mother and brother. Everyone was wearing expensive black clothes and somber faces. Her brother offered his hand, and she took it with relief. Unlike her, the town loved Kip. He was everybody's son, no matter how much ruckus or trouble he caused. They had always shrugged it off—Kip being Kip.

"I'm gonna be sick," she announced as they boarded the yacht.

Her mother tucked a strand of Caty's hair behind her ear, soothing her. "You'll be fine." That was her mother's idea of comforting her children. *You will be fine; just fake it for a little while.*

"Isn't this unsanitary? Spreading ashes in the ocean? What about the fish? What if they eat it?" She cringed at the thought of eating fish nourished by someone else's ashes.

Kip smothered a laugh, and she glared at him. "Why can't we do a normal burial?"

"Because this is what he wanted," Kip pointed out. "Everything in this yacht is what he wanted. Including you."

Caty winced. "I'm not sure about that."

"If he could get the whole town on the yacht, you know he would have loved it."

"Maybe I should just wait at Casa Isabella." Caty bit her lip and looked as the crew prepared to leave the dock. She looked around the yacht, and at the people on it. It wasn't a big crowd, mostly Sarge's patrons who were closest to him.

She felt completely out of place.

She thought about leaving, but then the anchor lifted, and they were off. She didn't want to cause a scene more than what her coming home had done. It took the last of her savings, and she knew she wouldn't be flying back home spontaneously anymore.

When Kip had called, she'd realized how much she missed home—if this was even home.

Jimmy booked her flight while Lucian helped her pack. It was all a blur, and only now that she was staring at the horizon did she understand how poignant the moment was.

Sarge was dead. San Juan as she knew it wouldn't be the same anymore.

In her periphery, she saw Madeline heading toward her. She had a black pashmina wrapped around her shoulders, and huge, dark sunglasses covered half her face. Of course, Caty had known that Madeline would be here. She was Sarge's prodigy, and she seemed to be truly grieving.

"Don't do it," Kip said before she could take a step forward.

"Why?" she answered.

"I don't know—it just doesn't seem like a smart idea to piss Maddy off. Especially when she can throw you right out into the ocean."

Caty smirked. "She can't take me. Her arms are too tiny to pick me up."

Kip laughed, and she joined in, but it didn't take long for others to glare at them.

Kip smiled at them politely before making his exit. "All right, but in case you need backup."

She squeezed his hand and knew he had her back. Caty turned to her mother, who was watching Madeline approach. "Mom, can I have a minute with Madeline when you're done greeting her?"

Her mother looked surprised but agreed. She welcomed Madeline with two kisses on the cheek. "Maddy, darling, I'm so sorry for your loss."

"Thank you, Mrs. Villamor," Madeline answered, clutching her arms at her waist. "He was the best mentor."

Caty's mom smoothly added, "I'm sure you'd like to chat with Catalina."

Madeline's lips tightened before she turned to Caty. "Yes, of course."

"Well, I'll leave you to it." Caty's mom turned and left quickly.

Caty felt a lump in her throat, but she swallowed, took a deep breath, and faced Madeline. She was like a Modigliani painting come to life. Wearing a black dress with dark lips pinched tight, she was lovely, even for a grieving mentee.

What should she say first? *I'm sorry?* How do people comfort each other at funerals without sounding like a broken record? She stood quietly and didn't say anything for a moment until she couldn't stand the silence.

"I'm sorry."

Madeline remained motionless, as if she had earplugs in and hadn't heard anything. She was basically a still life painting planted in front of Caty.

"Sarge was . . . well." How could she put Sarge into words? "He was always the life of the party. He would have loved this, though he might have said the music was too slow."

Madeline was still doing a stellar job of remaining stoic.

"Okay, so, nice to see you." Caty took a step back.

Madeline cleared her throat. "Would you come by the house after?"

"What?" Was she serious? Are they going to be friends? Are they going to bond over this?

Madeline removed her sunglasses and showed that she had been crying.

"Better if you're not too late."

Caty was stumped. Had they had this conversation before? Had she missed something?

"I'd like to redecorate our basement, and your stuff is in the way," Madeline said stiffly, raising an eyebrow.

"You want me to help you clean up?"

"Your luggage," Madeline spat.

"*You're shitting me.*"

Madeline's mouth twitched. "Do it before my husband arrives."

"Where is he, anyway?" She craned her neck. She had been wondering . . . Not that she was chasing him anymore.

Did she love Otto? Maybe. She had loved the idea of having him, had even been obsessed with it. Maybe he was even her first love, the man she imagined all men should be when she was still a teenager. He was charming and attractive, and he seemed to be fond of her, even before things got romantic. It had just been . . . *zap*. Like being struck by lightning.

But in hindsight, she realized, being struck by lightning also meant getting burned.

"Wouldn't you like to know." Madeline's eyes flashed.

"That's no—" she struggled to explain. Did everyone forget that she had been a friend of Otto's too? Before she screwed it up and fell for him? "I was just wondering, for you. I don't know—don't answer that."

"You know, when you left, I thought that would be it, problem solved. But you're not the only problem." Madeline's lips curled, finally wiping away the sad look on her face. "There will always be someone else. Not prettier, not better, but loose enough."

"Hey!" Caty knew she'd raised her voice. Everyone seemed to turn toward her, and she caught Kip's eye. She shook her head.

Madeline put her glasses on, settling back to her stoic face. "Pick up your shit, or I'll burn it."

Caty took a deep breath. "I'll have someone pick it up."

Madeline answered, "He comes home tomorrow."

"Well, thanks for the information, but you can relax, okay? I'm not going to see him again, unless we meet accidently on the street or something."

"I'm not worried about you." Madeline turned away. "He's already preoccupied with some girl from the city."

Despite herself, she actually felt sad for Madeline. "Oh, Maddy."

"Men are all the same," she concluded, as if she had learned a hard truth. "Right? Doesn't matter if you're together, doesn't matter if you're married. They're all just gonna do the same thing, right?"

Madeline was shaking, obviously trying not to explode by telling her more. It must be hard for her to admit that her picture-perfect life was anything but. Caty dared to reach for her hand. "Maddy, no."

She pulled her hand away, of course. In her eyes, Caty was one of them. Caty understood, but at that moment she wished Madeline could believe she was not the enemy.

"I'm sorry he did this to you," she said.

Caty had known Otto since she was a child. Once she would have said, *But that's just him,* as if that was an acceptable reason for his behavior. Now she knew it was a shitty excuse and an even shittier thing to do.

Caty wanted Madeline to know that Otto was a grade A jerk, and that there were better people out there. People who wouldn't cheat, who wouldn't make her feel left out and replaced, people she could believe in and trust.

But she understood that this was still new and fresh for Madeline and nothing she could say right now would be received well.

Madeline stepped back. "Fine, I'll have my driver drop off your stuff."

She walked away, and Caty realized that would be best. From a distance, her brother kept an eye on her, as he had promised.

The rest of the funeral was strange, but it was what Sarge had planned. They spread his ashes; the people grieved and told stories, ate some food, and drank some wine. Caty had been looking around the group, trying to recognize the faces. She remembered some, others not so well. She kept searching, hoping for . . . something, or someone.

They watched the clouds turn from orange to pink to violet. She savored that feeling before they had to return to shore, to the town and its people, to their own lives, without Sarge.

"That was . . . nice," Caty said.

"Your father would have loved that," their mother said.

Kip grimaced. "No. Dad hated being on the water."

"I meant the sunset, not spreading his ashes. God, no."

Caty laughed; she felt a bit lighter in spite of the somber mood. She looked on as everyone got into cars and started out for Casa Isabella, leaving the port empty. She realized that she liked being here because of her family, but she'd always felt like she never truly belonged in San Juan. She was always looking for a way out, to get somewhere else, to be in a place where she felt more like herself.

Standing next to her family, Caty knew that being home was never really about where she was. It was about whom she was with.

Her life suddenly felt like the empty lot, stripped clean and barren. She had no idea what to do next, and judging from Hans's dismay about her sudden absence, she wasn't positive she'd have a job when she got back to New York. How hard could it be to replace her?

At least she still had Lucian and Jimmy.

And her mother and Kip.

She had some people who did stay with her. *The ones you didn't scare away,* she thought and then shook off that idea.

Her mother was already in the back seat when she called to Caty, "You all right, honey?"

"Yeah," Caty answered, and joined her in the car.

They drove through familiar roads, places she used to play in, the school she went to, the street she and her friends rode bikes on, her dad's old office, that place where all the town parties were held.

Caty had stopped feeling homesick for San Juan a long time ago, but watching the scenery go by, she finally understood that all along, she'd been yearning for a home.

sixteen

Elan would've taken his mother home right after mass, but she had a birthday party to go to. So he watched her talk to her friends before they left for the party. Gia left as soon as the mass ended to fetch Abby from her playdate. She'd told him they could keep meeting on Sundays to spend more time with their mother.

He didn't insist but was glad to hear it, knowing full well that his sister was mostly parenting alone until her husband returned for a few months. Then he'd go back to his work on a freighter, traveling all over the world.

He heard his mother and her friends talk about him, even if he was standing right there. Elan was used to his name coming up every time an old friend's single daughter was coming to visit. He would usually smile and shrug it off.

His mother did the same—laugh at the idea and not fully commit to it. Elan thought that was because his mother wasn't ready to let him go just yet, and he knew why. He was the only one she had left. Sure, there was her group of friends, but she lived alone in the house that he and Gia had grown up in.

Elan had suggested that she live with someone—a friend, a helper—or if she ever met someone and fell in love again, he and Gia would be fine with that. But his mother insisted she was okay and she actually liked being alone.

When the group got ready to carpool, he checked with her again, just in case. "You don't need a ride back?"

She shook her head. "I'll ride with Carmen. I'll be fine." She squeezed his arm. "Will you be all right driving by yourself?"

He thought it was funny, being asked that. "Yes. Of course."

His mother cupped his cheek and patted it. "You look like you need some company. You could still come with us. I heard Tina's niece will be there."

She rolled her eyes when she said it, and that made Elan laugh. She never pushed hard about setting him up with girls, but she didn't stop trying either. Even if she couldn't present the idea with a straight face.

"I'm fine," he assured her, fishing his car keys out of his pocket. "I'll see you next week."

She nodded and smiled as he walked to his car.

"If you need to miss a weekend, that's okay too," she added. "Gia called me the other day to schedule a weekend with Abby."

Elan paused, looked his mother in the eyes, and thought there must be more to this. Before he could discuss it, his mother waved and rode away in the van with her friends.

He opened the door and got in but didn't start the car immediately. Elan watched as the women all left the parking lot eventually. The empty lot reminded him of how free he was for the rest of the day and how heavy and overwhelming that suddenly felt.

He sat in his car and felt his freedom but didn't know what to do with it.

When his phone rang, Elan stared at the name before picking up. It was Jules.

He answered the call and tried to listen to her passing on information so quickly he could barely catch up. Of course, it

was about Caty, and it sucked that it was back to this—finding
out things about her from secondary sources.

"I just thought I'd let you know."

"Thanks," was all he said.

"Should we expect you?"

It took him awhile to answer; the word was at the tip of his
tongue, but he couldn't let go of it yet.

"Elan?" Jules sounded worried.

"Did she ask for me?"

"Well . . . no. But—"

"Is she okay?"

"Yes, but—"

"Then no."

Caty laid the hydrangeas she'd picked from the Coronados'
garden on the table, getting ready to use the floral scissors. It
was the day after Sarge's funeral, and despite the previous night's
successful party at Casa Isabella, the town was somber.

She was thinking about doing a photo shoot just for the
sake of keeping busy and being productive while she was in
town. She had to leave sometime soon, but she honestly didn't
know which would be worse—staying in her hometown or
going back to the city where she wasn't welcome.

So Caty decided to play with the flowers and make a
centerpiece for the Coronados so they could enjoy the blooms.
Alone in the house, she worked in silence, humming an annoying
song she'd heard on the radio. Kip was at work, and their mother
was having lunch with the ladies of the Tourism Club.

She started cutting stems and placing them in a vase.
Hydrangeas were pretty easy to arrange; she had done it plenty

of times before, but today it felt like she was relearning things in slow motion.

When she was done and satisfied with what she created, Caty decided to walk back to the Coronados' to deliver the centerpiece. She needed to walk. Needed to do something. Needed to not think about things.

She buzzed at the gate. Much to her surprise, Juliana opened it.

"Hey. No work?" Caty guessed.

"Had to pick up something I forgot." She eyed the flowers in Caty's hand. "What's up?"

"Just dropping these off for your mom."

Juliana took the vase and reminded Caty, "She's with your mom. For lunch."

"Right." Caty had been forgetting things lately. Maybe she had just stopped paying attention to every detail. She felt tired thinking about it.

"Caty?" Juliana called. "Are you okay? Do you want to come in for a minute? I have time."

Caty hadn't been in the Coronados' house since she and Juliana both moved out of San Juan. It was a long time ago, but looking around the house and at the familiar room, her heart softened.

"How are you holding up?"

She followed the sound of Juliana's voice, a little bit disorientated.

"About Sarge, I mean."

"Oh," Caty gulped. She was fine, she guessed. "I'm okay."

"You want anything? Water? Have you eaten?"

She raised her hand and chuckled. "I'm good."

Juliana studied her for a moment. "How long are you planning to stay?"

Caty answered, "Not sure yet," and she followed Juliana over to the couch.

"Do you like what they did to this room?" Juliana tried again.

Caty knew Juliana was trying to make her talk. She probably seemed out of it, so she looked around the room and assessed it. They had redecorated, gotten rid of the chunky, old wooden furniture and replaced it with plush sofas in bold red.

"Who picked the color?"

"Mom," Juliana sighed.

"It's clashing with the walls," Caty noted. "Is she planning to repaint?"

"No, but I'm going to suggest it now."

Caty appreciated the fact that Juliana still had faith in her judgment, even about small things like this.

"How are you and Kip? Did he do something stupid? Be honest."

"What?" Juliana laughed. "No. Not yet. Not today."

They laughed, remembering how they had talked and laughed about boys in school. At first it had been weird that Juliana and Kip were together, but it was okay now that she finally understood they really were serious.

"How's New York?"

"It's . . ." Despite feeling as if she didn't belong, Caty was still enthusiastic about New York. It was her dream city. "Great. You ever think about visiting?"

"Actually, Kip and I were planning to," Juliana answered.

"Well, make it soon, 'cause I'm not sure how long I'll last there." It was supposed to be a joke, but it sounded real.

"You're thinking about moving again?"

Caty shrugged. "I might have to. But don't get me wrong, I don't want to leave New York."

"I can't imagine you would," Juliana snorted. "Ever since we were kids, all you've talked about is New York. Are you Samantha-ing it up there?"

"God, that's such a high standard." Caty rolled her eyes, giggling at the *Sex and the City* reference. "It's just not how I always imagined it would be."

"Isn't that how it always is?"

"I water this guy's plants, answer his phone, and pick up his dry cleaning." Caty frowned. "So far, I'm replaceable in New York."

"But that wasn't what you intended to do when you went there, was it?"

"No." She laughed. "I wanted to be something. Do something. Create beautiful things."

"And you're not doing any of that?"

"I made a cactus bloom," Caty replied, feeling a little proud. "Man, those suckers can be a pain. But they're pretty neat as props."

Juliana laughed. "You're still you, Caty. You can't be replaced. No one can ever be you."

Caty paused, bowed her head, and took in the words. "Thanks, Jules."

Juliana gave her a curious smile, brows meeting. "Jules? When did you ever call me that?"

Never. But Elan does. "It's your name, isn't it?"

Juliana considered. "Yeah. Well, I like it better than my full name, so stick with it."

Caty nodded, and a comfortable silence fell between them. She heard Juliana take in a breath before asking, "So, I'm not sure if I should ask, but whatever happened with Elan when he visited New York?"

"Why, what'd he tell you?"

"He hasn't said a thing. I mean, Elan and I don't really talk about our personal lives so much, but a souvenir would have been nice."

"He didn't get any," Caty recalled, even if she was working hard these days *not* to remember. But it was hard—every day she walked the same streets they had, rode the same train, had her bagel in the morning, frequented DUMBO at night. "Sorry, he had very little time."

"Oh, yeah," Juliana nodded. "Sucks that his mom was rushed to the hospital again, huh?"

The color drained from Caty's face; Juliana noted the shock and bit her lip. "He didn't tell you."

Caty coughed and cleared her throat. "No, he mentioned there was an emergency. I just didn't ask about it."

"Why not?"

Because that's personal, she defended herself. But then again, was it more personal than the things he'd already told her about his father? Maybe there was only so much he could give, and she couldn't decide if it was enough.

Caty gave Juliana a weak smile. "If he wanted to tell me, he would have."

She agreed, giving Caty a nod. Caty could tell that Juliana had something on her mind and wasn't ready to share it.

"Is his mom okay?"

Juliana nodded.

Good. She could never forgive herself if she had broken up with the guy at the same time something awful was happening to his mother. Well, she didn't even break up with him, not really, no matter what Jimmy and Lucian said.

Juliana sighed. "Are you guys—?" She didn't finish the question. How could Caty answer when she didn't even know herself?

"I don't know."

Juliana laughed. "Okay, well, that's—"

"Not ideal, I know," Caty ended the sentence for her.

"We kinda thought you guys were . . ." She gestured with two fingers twined around each other. "The visit didn't help?"

"God, no. If anything, it only confused me more."

"Why?"

"Because," she sighed, "trust me to like unavailable men."

"He's not unavailable." Juliana paused for a beat. "I think?"

"Is he seeing someone else here?" She just needed to know, she realized.

"No." Juliana laughed. "Quite the opposite. He has always been that way. He's available but unavailable."

"I don't understand?"

"Come to think of it, I don't either." Juliana started to say something else, paused, and then started all over again. "I used to have a crush on him in school, 'cause he was just one of those guys all the girls like. He's nice, he's smart, he looks good. Sort of a no-brainer."

Caty nodded, grinning. She wondered if Elan knew about Juliana's old crush. She also wondered how he would react now if he found out about it.

"I've never seen him with anyone, and it's not like women didn't try. He seemed open to the idea, but somehow things just didn't follow through."

"You mean *he* didn't follow through." Which made sense. She gave herself a mental high five, a pat; *I knew it!*

"I don't know enough. It's not like we talked about our relationships. We were more like study buddies," Juliana explained.

"He was in love with you. Did you know that?"

"Oh God, no," Juliana gasped, blushing in spite of herself.

"He was when I met him."

Juliana sighed. "Maybe he felt something, but I don't think he was ever in love with me."

Caty pursed her lips. "What makes you so sure?"

"Because, Catalina, and you should know better." Jules paused dramatically. "When you're in love, everything seems urgent. Everything has to be *now*. You have to be with them *now*. You have to know *now*. You get what I mean?"

She did. Didn't she act that way whenever she felt something for a guy? Hadn't she made her dad worried sick when she'd she snuck out to be with a boy she was infatuated with? Didn't she always find a way to get the attention she wanted from boys? Hadn't she risked being caught by Madeline just because she needed to see Otto?

"Elan and I knew each other for a long time, and we've never had that sense of urgency. We were comfortable. We got along. I like him, but as a friend." Her voice was loud and clear, and it sounded like a message especially for Caty.

It was petty to bring it up again, especially since Elan had been straightforward about being over Juliana, but she couldn't stop double-checking facts.

"When Kip left for Toronto, did you ask him to move back for you?"

"No," Juliana answered. "That was his decision."

Caty pouted. "So it's like what Lucian said. Someone has to be the braver one."

"Sure? That sounds sensible."

But her brother, Kip, had always been the reckless one. He was the one who did drastic things, like moving to another country just for a chance with a girl.

"But I was already sure of him before that. I just wasn't so brave in the beginning," Juliana added. "So I don't know. I guess what I'm saying is this." She took a deep breath. "There's no *first* or *most* when it comes to love. None of that matters at the end of the day. What's important is that you both give and receive."

"Did Elan tell you that he used to play basketball?"

Juliana looked surprised, "Really? No."

Caty smirked, confirming to herself that he had shared something with her alone. "Not well. But yeah."

She thought it through. Despite what happened that night in New York and this information she just confirmed, it still felt as if she was at the edge, and no one was on the other side.

"I don't want to leave New York."

"No one said you have to," Juliana assured her. "Why did you think that? Unless . . ."

Juliana's eyes widened as she fully understood what Caty wasn't saying. She blurted out, "You were thinking about leaving New York because of him?"

"No," Caty asserted, looking away.

Juliana gasped, "Caty!"

"I wasn't, okay? It's just that New York is pretty shitty for me right now, and it's bursting my bubble."

Juliana didn't respond, and Caty looked at her closely, afraid of what she'd see in her eyes.

"Stop it," Caty barked.

"Come on! You haven't even told me about that night you guys disappeared on my parents' wedding anniversary!"

"Nothing to tell."

She teased, "That's not what he told me."

Caty leaned forward. "If he said anything about sleeping in, I will cut off his tongue."

"You guys slept together?"

Caty huffed, leaned back. "I hate you right now."

Juliana laughed. "He never told me anything. That guy tells nothing to anyone. Except that one time he helped me on a test and saved my ass."

Caty narrowed her eyes. "He tells nothing to anyone? Even you?"

"He's like a ziplock bag. Shut tight. Except maybe with you?"

Caty faked a laugh and settled on her side of the couch. Juliana stayed put, smiling at her like this was the best day of her life. "So you like him," she concluded.

Caty shrugged a yes, even if the answer was obvious. She knew it, had even told Elan, and she wasn't embarrassed about it.

"And I know he likes you, 'cause he's been here a lot lately."

"In your house?"

"In San Juan," Juliana corrected. "It's like he's gathering intel on you."

Caty covered her face. "Why here? Why didn't he go to Toronto? There are much nicer memories of me there."

Juliana reached for her arm. "Hey, we have nice things to say about you here too."

Caty smiled back. Maybe it was true. Maybe her life here wasn't as horrible as she'd always thought it was. "Thanks."

"Plus, whatever he heard from the others, he doesn't seem to like you any less."

"He's not in his right mind," Caty joked. It was so much easier to be self-deprecating than to agree with what Juliana was trying to tell her.

Caty laughed nervously. "Did you tell him I'm not the easiest person to hold on to? I'm loud; I'm a little out there. I throw tantrums—I like being spoiled. I'm highly allergic when it comes to talking about things I'd rather not think about."

"Like about leaving New York so you can be with him?"

"And I live too far away," Caty finished. She looked up at the ceiling and noted that the chandelier had to go. It didn't match the new couch. But she was just evading the truth. "I think he's the only one who ever knew this much about me and still hasn't given up."

"Did you want him to?"

"I did kind of push him there," she said, not exactly proud of it. "I haven't been talking to him much these days."

"Why not?"

"Because we live far away, and we're naive to think we can keep the relationship alive, don't you think? I'm never gonna leave New York. He clearly needs to stay here—he's got a good job, and his family is here."

"Maybe he's in love with you too."

Caty tilted her head. "Too?"

Juliana gave her a look.

"Fine. You won't let that go."

"What are you afraid of?"

"I keep wondering what's gonna make him raise the white flag." Caty frowned. "Because if we do try again, it's gonna be hard. It's already hard for two people to be together, but to be apart while trying to make the relationship work? What's the point of it all? It's too cruel."

Juliana took in her answer with a nod, and Caty realized she had finally spoken out loud some of the thoughts she had been dealing with on her own. It felt cruel, like a joke the universe had played on her. It had found someone for her whom she actually wanted to be with, but that person was thousands of miles away.

"I don't think that's really the problem here," Juliana suggested. "The real question is: why do you still think he'll eventually give up on you?"

"Well," Caty said, almost choking on her words, "everyone's got a breaking point. Some can just tolerate more than others."

"I don't think Elan just tolerates you," Juliana retorted. "But I mean, if he still makes you feel that way, then maybe he didn't do his job."

Caty's breath hitched, and she exhaled loudly. "Which is?"

"Making you feel secure enough in your relationship."

Was that it? She had doubts, of course. She was riddled with them every night. She kept going around in circles, one doubt after the other. In previous relationships, she'd had doubts too, but having the person around made it easier to work things out. Being with them usually eliminated the doubts. And the body language she could see, instead of just words, was deeply important to her.

She shook her head to get rid of the thoughts. "Maybe if we both lived in the same city—"

"But that's just it, Caty," Juliana interrupted. "You don't. So what are you guys gonna do about it?"

Nothing, she thought. That's just how it is, and it doesn't work.

"So, you're telling me the only thing that's stopping you from being with the person you love is that he lives in another country?"

"Okay, calm down with the word *love,*" Caty warned. "And you're making it sound so simple."

"But it is," Juliana insisted. "You've got the problem figured out; you just need to think of the solutions. Distance aside, how do you feel about him anyway?"

Caty frowned. "You know."

"I don't," Juliana persisted. "I just kind of assumed, but you never really said it."

Caty almost shouted, "I want to be around him all the time, okay? I miss him so much that I started leaving my phone at home so I wouldn't have to talk to him."

"Why did you stop talking to him anyway?"

"Because," Caty felt her eyes water, "it isn't fair. For him. For me. We've created this little bubble, and it's nice, but that's all it is. It's a bubble. An escape. And I want more, Jules."

Juliana just wouldn't stop smiling, and that threw Cathy off, so she tuned it down a bit. "I mean, I want things. Real, tangible things. I can't do vague anymore."

"There's nothing wrong with that," Juliana replied. "You don't think he could give you those things?"

"I don't know. Don't get me wrong, I feel a certain calm when I'm with him. It's a strange feeling. My heart is . . . I don't know, settled. Full. When I'm with him, it's quiet. I feel . . ."

"Safe?"

Caty stopped. She remembered how she used to walk home at night thinking of him and feeling as if she wasn't alone. He was with her during that walk, her head filled with his stories throughout that day.

She recalled how she felt that night when she slept in his arms and woke up still wrapped up with him, like she was meant to be there. That was why she never forgot it. That was the feeling she'd been trying to replicate with other people but couldn't.

She even remembered how it was that first time she saw him in the driveway and how she ran out to him, yelling, "*Wait!*"

She felt safe.

Eventually, she had recognized that with him she felt at home, in spite of the distance she was so worried about. She believed in him.

She actually trusted him.

Caty gasped and met Juliana's eyes. She seemed to understand what was going on, what had just happened, what Caty was thinking.

She smiled, reached her hand out to tap on Caty's. "So maybe he did do his job."

"I need to—"

"Talk to him? God, finally. It's getting ridiculous, what you two are doing."

"Can you drive me to him?"

"Mmm." Juliana tilted her head. "I have a feeling he'll be here. Any day now."

"*Any day?*" Her eyes widened. "I can't wait that long!"

. Juliana leaned back, a smug smile on her face. "See? Urgency."

seventeen

Just home from his ride, Elan wondered, *What else do people do these days?* He thought about going out again, just to fill in the time, but he was also comfortable inside, so he just took a shower and decided to stay in.

Then the phone rang, and he suspected it was Gia. He read the name on the screen and stopped short.

It didn't register right away, as if his brain lagged, forgot how to interpret the letters. At the same time, *he knew, he got it,* he understood what it was, what this meant.

Elan stared at his screen for another moment, eyes wide, his thumb hovering.

Then it stopped ringing. Her name disappeared from the screen.

Fuck. *Fuckfuckfuckfuckfuck.*

He could call her, right? She wanted to talk, now.

Muttering another curse, he worked his thumb furiously to call her back. Elan brought the phone to his ear and waited for it to ring. After a few painful seconds, he finally heard the call go through, and all he could think of was whether he would hear more than rings. *Did she change her mind? Was it just a mistake? Was she ever going to pick up?*

On the fifth or sixth ring, he leaned his arms on his knees, covered his face with a hand and bit his lip, thinking, *Come on, come on, come on.*

Then a click and silence.

He could hear her breathe, but she didn't speak.

Maybe that was good. He had so much to say. Words would pour out of his mouth, but he waited breathlessly. *Wasn't he glad he'd had years of practice in holding things back?*

"Where have you been?" she asked.

"Right here," Elan said, welcoming her back to the tiny bubble they barely had. He'd held the fort, kept watch in case she came back.

And she had.

He heard Caty sigh but didn't say anything.

"You know what? This is better. Let me talk for a bit," Elan started again, even if he didn't really know where to begin. The phrases and words were circulating around his head.

Since his talk with Gia the other day, he'd thought again about everything Caty had said. Gia's questions hung in the air: *Did she know? Did you tell her?*

He thought he had, but maybe he hadn't been as direct as he should have been. He had wanted the visit to be about more than just that night; he wanted it to go beyond that. He had to tell her that now.

If he did, and the situation was still the same—that she still chose to be with someone else—then he could still walk away without asking the questions that riddled him at night.

"I'm sorry," Elan decided to start with that. "I think I was angry."

He never said that word. He was scared of even thinking it. It was an ugly word for him, one he associated with the kind of person he didn't want to be. He'd forgotten that being angry is being human, that it was an emotion he was allowed to feel if he cared enough, if it mattered.

And this, *this* mattered. He cared about what happened to him and Caty.

Elan let out a heavy sigh and looked down at his feet. "When you said you started seeing somebody else that night, I got mad, or jealous, one of those things. I shouldn't have been upset because neither of us had said anything about not seeing other people. But I felt it."

"Oh," Caty sounded surprised.

"I realize that I'll probably ask a lot from you. I mean, this is hard." He thought about what it was like for her, on the other side. She was probably exhausted. *He exhausted her.* The whole setup was tiring. It involved a great deal of effort to keep connecting to a person who wasn't there physically.

"And frankly, you shouldn't have to wait for some guy to wake up." Elan remembered that particularly—Caty told him she was waiting but didn't want to keep doing it.

"Caty, that's not how you should feel about us. You shouldn't feel miserable. You should be taken out, treated well, kissed every day."

Maybe he shouldn't give her ideas about what the other guy should do, but he had to say it anyway. He meant it, although part of him was screaming, *It should be me.* He wanted it more than anything.

Elan used to think he would just have to try harder once he had it all figured out, but when was that gonna be? He now understood that he didn't have to sort it all out before acting. Time was running out, and wasn't that what he just said? *She shouldn't be waiting for a guy to wake up.*

In the past few days, he had shaken himself up, as if he had slapped himself in the face. It might have involved Gia's help too, but here he was, admitting that he needed to wake up.

"Wow, okay," she said, shock in her voice. "That's a lot to take in. We haven't even said hello."

"Right, sorry. Hello."

"Hello." He thought he heard a smile in her voice. "You said sorry *way* too many times."

"That's how sorry I am."

"For what again?"

"I don't know," his voice trailed. "Feeling . . ."

"Mad? Jealous?" Caty offered, "Anything else?"

"Miserable. Mostly."

"I'm sorry." Her turn to say it. "You should never feel sorry for that."

Then it was quiet.

"Well, isn't this in the running for the most depressing conversation we've ever had," Elan commented.

"The last one was actually more depressing," she reminded him. He cringed at the thought of how he had sniped at her.

"I know, I'm—"

She interrupted before he could say sorry again. "We started it all wrong. Should we try again?"

"You want me to call you back?"

"No."

"Right." He faced the door. *She was here in San Juan.* They were in the same latitude, the same time zone. "I'll drive to you."

"I have a better idea," Caty said. His eyes opened wide when he heard knocks on the door. "Open the door."

eighteen

Caty stood at the door, still on the phone, waiting for it to open.

It was a lot for one phone call. Her ears were burning, her heart was racing, and she was pretty sure she was close to crying. One blow and she'd tip over.

The door opened, and her eyes met his.

"Hi," was the first thing she said, over the phone. "You cut your hair."

"I did," he replied, running a hand through his hair.

"It's . . ." Her eyes roamed over him, hungry to notice the details. What did she miss? One whole month of not seeing his face. She marveled at the sensation of familiarity, nostalgia hitting her in the chest, despite the fact that she was right in front of the person she missed. *He didn't change,* she recognized, and when he smiled at her, her heart warmed. "I like it."

Elan was the first to address the fact that they were still talking over the phone. "Should we stay on our phones?"

"Just for a sec," Caty answered. She wasn't done yet. She smiled at him, dwelling on the fantastic feeling of seeing him again, reacquainting herself with what she already knew, reveling in the pleasure of wanting to get to know this person again, and again.

Elan leaned on the door frame, one brow raised. "It's just that—someone's at the door."

"Serial killer?"

He laughed, and she watched his eyes crinkle and his lips spread. Laugh lines showed on his face. "No, some girl."

"She hot?"

"Smokin'."

Caty blushed, although she had orchestrated it. "You should make out with her then."

He hesitated. "Can I do that?"

"You might need to assess the situation first."

"Right. Well," he crossed his hand over his chest. "Everything is the same with me. Exactly where I was the last night we met. Except I'm the idiot who didn't tell her exactly how he felt."

Her eyes met his, and she could hear her heart beating as if it was right next to her ears, thumping, drumming.

"I adore her," he said, flat out. "I'd hijack projects for a chance to get on a trip that would allow me to see her even for a day."

Caty held her breath and felt bad that she had lied to him. But she would tell him *now*, correct it *now*.

"I live for her."

"What?"

Elan raised his hand. "Not that I would die if she wasn't around. It's about the way I live when she's with me. Everything around me feels more alive. And it's not a coincidence, it's not something else, it's just her. She brings that into my life."

Caty couldn't find her voice, even when she already had so much to say.

"I'm in love with her."

She looked away to press the end button on the phone, swallowing hard. She took a deep breath before looking back at him.

All her life, Caty had wanted someone to look at her the way Elan was looking at her this moment. Yet she didn't know what to do next.

"Too real?" he asked, putting his phone down.

She took the first step toward him. "Fucking kiss me already."

"What about that guy you're seeing?" he said cautiously.

"Who?" *Right.* That. The lie. Biting her in the ass just as she thought.

"You told me you were—"

"I made him up," she spat out. She just had to do it that way, no need to embellish a lie with more lies. "There's no one else."

His brows furrowed, and his eyes asked her to tell him more.

"I only had you on this tiny screen. It had gotten so pathetic that I would wake up with my eyes glued to the phone and fall asleep while I was still holding it. I was too attached to my phone. I needed to unplug. There was just too much happening in my real life, and then there was you—someone who's *real* but somewhat unreal—"

"You made him up?"

That was all he took away from everything she'd said? Yes, she was awful for what she did, she got it. "Yes."

Elan opened his mouth but could only come up with, "Why?"

"Because," she hung her head, "I wanted to stop this."

He leaned on the door frame and tilted his head.

Caty took a step toward him and saw his hand reaching out to hers, so she took it and let him pull her in. She landed in his arms, both hands resting on his chest.

"*This?*"

"God, don't be dense," Caty complained. She hadn't asked Jules to drive her all the way here to be cute about this. Hell, she hadn't flown back and drained her savings to miss what she needed to hear. To not say what she needed to say. "You know what this is. Everything you did was leading up to this. You were making me fall in love with you. And surprise, it worked. Damn it. No, damn *you*."

Elan grabbed her face and kissed her, finally, both his hands angling her face to kiss her deeper. A tear rolled off her cheek as the warmth of his touch and his kiss spread through her body.

He pulled back, leaned his forehead on hers, and breathed in.

"I miss you," she whispered, holding on to his wrists. "You're right in front of me, and I still miss you."

She anticipated their next kiss. She was due for one more, right? He couldn't kiss her like that and not keep going. She would just fall apart, right at this very doorstep.

But the kiss didn't come. In fact, he was letting go of her. Caty looked up to see why he had stopped, why he was pulling away, hands frantically holding on to his arms. Their eyes met, and a little shiver ran down her spine.

Her lips parted.

He kicked the door, and it swung back. "Come in," he finally said, his voice strained.

Caty would have just walked past him, but she didn't. Again, she wasn't here to be cute. She was here to get what she wanted, so she threw her arms around his neck and pushed him in while she kissed him.

Elan rested his head in the crook of Caty's neck. He pressed another kiss on her collarbone as her arms enveloped him.

Caty laughed, tickled by his breath when his lips traveled up her throat to her ear, his weight right above her. They'd been holding each other for a while, since they kicked that door shut and discarded each other's clothing.

It was a blur, but it also had clarity, a sense of right that settled in her stomach.

Caty ran her hand through his hair. "Your room is very you."

"What do you mean?"

"It's so . . ." Her eyes took in the blank walls, devoid of photos, posters, or any reference of the person living there. "Blank."

"Thanks?"

"No, I mean, you don't show off your stories." She gave him a smile. "Not to just anyone."

Elan barely moved from his position.

"I wish you had told me about your mom," she breathed out.

She felt Elan shift on top of her. "I know. I screwed that up."

"You didn't have to, if you're still not comfortable, but I think it would have helped me understand you better."

She felt saddened by how she did this. She did her fair share of self-sabotage before, but this one just took the cake. She made herself miserable. Even made him miserable. She would need to make it up to him so bad. "There were times I wished I could have just stopped. Called you. But maybe a part of me knew that it had to be more than a call."

"A call is preferred. A smoke signal is more than welcome. Morse code is accepted."

She laughed.

"So you flew back?"

"Well, Sarge."

"I heard," he said quietly. "Although, to be honest, I didn't really expect you to come."

She took a deep breath, "I know, I'm surprised myself. But I feel sad."

He looked down at her, letting his hand brush the hair at the top of her head.

"He was just Sarge, you know?" Her brows met, not sure where she was going. "He didn't do anything specifically malicious toward me. I think I just sort of hated him 'cause he represented things about the whole town that I didn't like."

Elan eased the wrinkle between her brows with his thumb.

"Then I just feel bad," Caty continued, "because when I got the call about his funeral, I saw it mainly as an opportunity to get back here and see my family. See you. Does that make me awful?"

He smiled. "Makes you human."

"An awful one."

He laughed, and that made her feel as if it was all right to laugh too.

"So yeah, I came home and thought maybe when I was here I could figure out how to fix the mess I made," she explained. "I wasn't really thinking this would happen."

"You weren't? I could have saved you a lot of time."

Caty rolled her eyes. "Oh, 'cause sex solves everything?"

"It doesn't, but it helps with the frustration," he joked.

"How come you didn't try to call me?" Caty asked.

Elan's laughter subsided, his face pulling into a frown. "Hang on. For the record, I didn't need you to do something more for me. I just needed you back."

"I thought about calling you. Tried to go through with it, but I thought you wouldn't like it if I did it too quickly. Might push you further away if I insisted. So I stepped back."

She thought about it and agreed. He really did understand her, despite spending so little time together. He was learning about her the whole time, while she kept convincing herself to reduce their relationship to nothing even when it was so important.

"I figured I could just talk to Lucian."

"What? How?"

Elan licked his lips. "Not every day. Just to see if you're doing all right. I called Riot! and asked for Lux."

She paused, her mouth agape. "You're serious."

"Made friends with that bartender. Jordan?"

Caty bit her lip.

"Did he really give you a free drink, or was I paying for nothing?"

She covered her face with her hands. "*Oh my god.*"

"Hey." Elan wrapped his fingers around her wrist. "Sorry. Was that too much?"

It was not. He had respected her space and allowed her to come to terms with it herself while he stood by. Caty kept her face covered. "You were doing all that even when you were mad?"

He didn't answer right away, so she peeked at him through her fingers. He laughed and pulled her hands off her face. "I was mad, but not at you, really. I was mad at the circumstances. And that's hardly a reason for me to care about you less."

She caressed his face as she leaned in, her forehead touching his. So patient. Like he said. "Thanks. That's . . . it's what I needed."

"So? Catch me up. Lucian was very brief with me."

She suspected this was because Lucian was being loyal to her, and she felt a pinch in her heart, missing him already. "It's not like I did a lot in that time. A month isn't that long."

"It was hell."

"I found a better coffee place. I started walking Hans's dog. And I shot some things for my friend Clara's website." Caty continued, "If it makes you feel better, I kinda hated it too."

That's when he propped himself up and looked at her. "You had a shoot? How did that go?"

"Well," she paused, "I haven't heard from her yet. But I haven't checked my e-mail since I got here."

She was about to say something else, but he grabbed her face and kissed her hard, as if he hadn't just spent the last hour kissing her. As if he never tired of it. "Check it now."

"Are you serious?" Caty bit her lip. "You want me to check my e-mail?"

Elan nodded.

"Way to kill the postcoital bliss."

"Just do it."

Caty leaned in to kiss him, and he obliged, but it was softer, tender.

"Okay." She cleared her throat. "But if I get bad news, you're gonna make up for it."

"Gladly." Elan rolled away so she could find her phone.

"Jeans?" he asked.

"Purse," she answered.

"I'm pretty sure that's still right by the door."

"Can I walk around here naked? No creepy neighbors?"

Elan sat up. "Go for it. I'll keep an eye on you."

"I'm sure," she snorted. Caty ran out of the room, and her purse was right where he said it would be by the door. She joined him under the covers.

She opened her e-mail. It took awhile to load, but when it did, there was a message from Clara. She tapped on it and began reading.

After awhile, he stroked her arms, and she figured it was because she hadn't said anything. She read the e-mail twice before she looked up at him. "Clara wants to work with me for a few more shoots, and there's an event she wants me to attend so she can introduce me to more people."

Elan pulled her in when she said, "Yay," or something like that. "That's great."

"Yeah," she agreed, settling down, letting her head slide back to his chest. "That is good."

"When is it?"

Caty winced.

"Let me guess. You actually have to be at the airport in about . . ." Elan checked the time.

"*Stop.*" She hit him playfully, but the short deadline seemed likely given the fact that they always left each other after a day. But she was already ready to e-mail Clara to let her know where she was. "It's in two weeks."

"So you really have to go back to New York."

"Do you think I should just . . . stay?"

"Weren't you at home in New York?"

"Maybe I'm not. You made me hate the city." Caty frowned.

Elan's brows met. "You don't hate New York."

"I do now," she said quickly, trying to hide that crack in her voice. "I hate that you're not there."

"Hey, I hate it too," Elan added, and that didn't help either. She hated how being in New York meant he couldn't be next to her, that he couldn't put his arms around her, like this. "But you love New York."

"I can love other things too," she reasoned. "I think New York is rejecting me."

"That's ridiculous; how can anyone reject you?"

She gave him a look.

He remembered the first time they met and how that went. "You're really not gonna let that one go, are you? How many times do I have to make it up to you?"

"For the rest of your life," Caty decided. She liked the sound of that. His whole life attending to her. "Just kidding. You've made it up to me plenty. Though I don't mind being made up to."

"Noted."

"But New York. I think we're not compatible after all."

"It's only been a couple of months," Elan reasoned. "And if there's anything you need to take away from our first night, it's that you always end up winning people over. I wasn't sure about you that day we met, but you pretty much never left my mind after that night."

"Because you blew it, that's why. It was all about your ego—admit it."

"It was not," he answered. "New York can't be that heartless. It'll warm up to you."

"If I go back to New York, we're back to square one," Caty pouted. "Look, I'm not gonna lie to you. I don't like long-distance relationships."

"Are there people who like them?"

"Be serious for a minute. I really—I can't keep talking to you on the phone."

"I know," he said quickly. "But our problem wasn't just that we live in different continents."

"Oh?"

"The problem was that we hadn't even decided what *this* is," Elan explained.

"And we have now?"

He propped himself up with his elbows and teased, "Oh, don't be dense."

Caty pinched him.

"We're in love, aren't we?" He sat up, suddenly serious.

So she sat up too, clutching the sheets. "Yeah?"

"And we want to be together."

"Yeah." *That, she wanted. She wanted it so bad.*

"Do you still think you're gonna change your mind about me?"

She paused, thought about it, then shook her head. "I don't think my mind decides these things anymore."

His brows met.

Caty bowed her head and laughed, "Coming up here to see you almost felt instinctive. A bit primal. I don't know. I just feel it; I can't describe it."

"I know." Elan leaned in, cupped her face, and kissed her again. He rolled her on her back and made her understand that he knew what she meant in *this* language.

Urgency. She had that.

When he pulled back, she sighed, bit her swollen lip, and then said, "So we go wherever the other one goes. Eventually."

Eventually. She took in the word, let it run through her and settle. Elan didn't say anything while she pondered.

"You know that sooner or later, we're gonna have to really sit down and sort this all out, right?"

"Yes," Elan nodded.

"It's gonna get boring." She rolled her eyes.

"Never with you, though."

"Would you consider living elsewhere?" Caty asked.

"Sure."

"But this has always been home for you."

Elan shrugged. "I'm starting to think home really isn't a place. Not particularly. It's a feeling. I think home is with you."

"That's weird. I thought the same thing earlier. Are we being rash?"

"Could be," Elan answered.

Caty pursed her lips. "Not helpful."

Elan reached over to her, rubbed her arms with his hand. "Let's see. Two people met. They got to know each other."

"Sure, if that's what you want to tell people. Let's keep it PG." She shifted to lay her head on his chest.

He laughed, squeezed her shoulder as he rested his chin on her head. "They fell in love, so they chose to be together."

She kissed his chest and smiled. "When you put it that way, doesn't seem irrational at all."

"We could just be the smartest people in the world."

nineteen

They'd been here before.

The first time they met. She was asleep in the passenger seat, and he had to wake her up, Elan remembered. It wasn't that long ago. He'd stared at her while she slept, trying to figure out how to wake her up. What to do after that.

How to say goodbye.

Maybe he was just struggling to let her go.

Today wasn't so different. She looked out the window as they drove. It was a quiet drive, but it wasn't awkward. They'd learned how to sit in silence comfortably and not be concerned about filling it.

He reached for her hand at times, and she would take it, cradle it in her lap, press her cheeks against it.

They'd had two weeks. It was the most time they had spent together since they met. She stayed in his apartment when he went to work, did some of her work on his laptop, made a mess of rearranging his apartment when ideas struck her, even in the middle of the night. He loved it.

Elan adored seeing her bent down, completely absorbed in her projects. He loved to sit back and watch her do her thing, and he welcomed her back whenever she was ready.

And when she came back to him, he felt it so. Caty gave him the same attention she did with her work—doting on him and making sure he was all right.

He was more than all right.

Elan was great. He was *happy,* as much as that word could mean. He had dreaded the day she had to leave again, but surprisingly he felt all right.

When they reached the airport terminal, he parked on the side and faced her.

"Are you sure about this?" she asked.

She was asking him, again, when it really should be him asking her. "Are you?"

Caty rolled her eyes. "You're putting this all on me."

"I'm not," Elan reasoned.

"I'm just saying," Caty started, "if we broke up because of this—"

"We're not breaking up. You need to stop thinking of that as a default. *We're not breaking up.* Okay?"

She smiled sheepishly. "Yes, okay, sorry. *Not breaking up,* new default, programming myself with it."

"I'm sure. You need to go back to New York," he repeated, even though it felt as if they'd gone through this before. "You love New York. When you start to talk about it, your face lights up. The other day, when we were having breakfast, all you talked about were bagels. *Bagels, Caty.*"

"And? I'm just saying there aren't enough good bagels here."

"I cannot listen to this again," he complained, but he was smiling. He was telling her to go, yet he was still smiling.

"You want me to go because I have this weird obsession with finding good bagels?"

"It's cute that you're doing that thing again." Elan unlocked the doors and stepped out of the car to get her luggage from the trunk.

She got out and suggested, "We could start a bakery."

Elan laughed as he pulled her luggage out. "Do you know how to bake?"

"No," she answered, flat out.

"Go back and do what you started out to do." He handed her the luggage.

"You overestimate me," Caty sighed, taking the handle from him. "Fine, I'll go back to New York. As you wish. I'll beg Hans for another chance and work extra hard, while I also make plans to take over the world."

She paused. "I'm already exhausted just thinking about it."

"You can do it," Elan responded, leaning forward to kiss her.

Caty leaned back. "Seriously, though."

He bit his lip. "Seriously?"

"Yeah," she nodded. She looked nervous, so he pulled her in for a hug.

Elan spoke, "Look, I didn't want to say it yet because it's not even the surest thing, but when I was in Philly, we went to this university. I got really interested in one of their programs. The place was nice. I really liked it."

"That sounds okay, but do they have a good team?" she asked, still embracing him.

"I'm thinking of applying."

Caty hit him playfully on the arm as she stepped out of the embrace. "Shut up. That's only, like, a two-hour drive?"

He laughed. "I'm not in yet."

"Of course you're gonna get in! You're, like, really smart. You were reciting things in your sleep, by the way. And it was all very impressive. I tried to write it down, but I couldn't keep up."

Elan was embarrassed. He didn't know that he talked in his sleep. How come nobody had told him?

"This is great," Caty kept on, her excitement building.

This was exactly why he hadn't wanted to tell her, yet. So he said, "We don't know that. Plus I have to apply for funding and—"

"*Shush,*" Caty interrupted, beaming at him. "It's a shot. Sometimes, that's all we need."

He looked her in the eyes, took in how happy she looked at that very moment, and decided that it was okay to have this. Some tiny hope they would be together again, a tentative deadline for their separation.

"Elan," she called his name. "I'm not being naive. We're going to hate each other for wanting to go through with this. It's going to be hard. We'll be soaking in frustration most of the time. It's like we're setting each other up for heartbreak by deciding to go through this."

"Great, I can't wait," he deadpanned. "There's a *but* in this speech, right?"

Caty laughed and rubbed her thumb on his cheek. "*But.*"

He smiled, taking her hand to kiss it.

"We're gonna make this work."

"Yeah?"

Caty leaned in and kissed him, then whispered, "*Yes,*" as she opened her mouth to deepen the kiss.

A loud honk could have broken up that kiss, but he was saying goodbye to his woman, so they could just find another place to unload their luggage, minimum time for parking in front of the terminal be damned.

Caty pulled away first, turned to the honking car, and screamed, "Just a second!"

Elan winced but laughed at it all. She returned to give him soft kisses before pulling away completely. She had her eyes closed as she sighed, "Okay, I'm going."

He leaned back on his car, hands in his pockets as he watched her go.

"Hey," he called.

She looked up, eyes hopeful, kind, and beautiful. Elan shuddered, like he did that first time, because she was looking at him, and he was looking at her, and they knew, even without the words, *they knew.*

But sometimes saying it out loud works too.

"I love you."

Caty's face broke into a grin, and it was hard for him not to do the same. If this was their new way of saying goodbye, then he liked it far better.

She mouthed the words back to him before finally heading to the doors.

Elan drove away, and he had to stop himself from looking at the passenger seat. He was confident that this time, they were not saying goodbye.

He'd told her he loved her, and she'd told him she loved him. The best thing was that he knew it was true.

EPILOGUE

TWO YEARS LATER

It was too early. The sky was a purple haze, the last remnant of night fighting to stop the sun from spreading its light.

She was awake but quiet, holding on to the arms wrapped around her. She'd always had trouble adjusting to the time difference when she was on the other side of the world, but she didn't want to move. If possible, she wanted to stay forever in this room, live in this bed, in this moment, in this embrace. She listened to him sleep, heard his breath, tried to memorize every detail as if they were scraps of food to take home.

They didn't see each other often. She still lived in a big city, and he'd stayed in his country. But he was always with her, wherever she was. She'd gone from someone who worried too much to someone who was secure in herself and what she had.

He gave her that.

In the dark, she felt his arms move, so she turned back to face him. They were both awake. They had awakened early, even before the sun, because they had no time to waste.

Elan tilted his head slowly to reward her with a smile. Caty had missed seeing his face, missed having him wrapped around her arms as much as she missed being wrapped up in his. He leaned in, grabbed her face, and kissed her hard. She returned his kisses with the same urgency and passion, because in that space, she felt most alive.

He slowed but lingered, nibbling at her lips until they were swollen and bitten. He left a trail of kisses on Caty's shoulders and neck, whispered sweet things in her ear, kissed it, told her he loved her once, maybe twice, and she believed it all, kissed him back, and told him she loved him too.

She wanted to wake up to all of this every day.

They settled in bed, listening to the sound of the waves crashing into the shore.

"I don't like being the bad cop, but it's time to go."

"No," she pleaded. "Five more minutes."

He craned his neck to check the clock. "You can sleep in the car."

Caty squeezed her eyes shut and hugged the covers.

"You can sleep on the plane," Elan suggested, pulling her hand.

"I don't like sleeping on planes."

"You can also sleep back home."

She groaned but sat up. *Home. Today was that day.* She'd prepared herself for it as much as she could. They had worked for this day for so long, made sacrifices, waited too long.

Caty raised her arms. "Help me, please. This bed won't let me go."

He laughed and grabbed her by the waist instead. "Is this how it's gonna be every morning?"

"If I say yes, would you change your mind?" She wrapped her legs around his hips as he carried her off the bed.

"Not at all."

So they were ready. The bags had been packed the night before, and they only needed to shower and get dressed. Elan and Caty grabbed breakfast on the way and drove to the airport, where they'd be meeting Gia.

Gia was there when they arrived, and she welcomed them both with hugs.

"How was the beach?"

"Great," Caty replied. Now she would be returning to the cold after her fix of sun and sea.

"Everything is packed?" Gia asked.

"Yes, we're good," Elan answered, putting the bags on the cart.

"Okay, then."

He paused when everything was loaded. Caty took over and started to push the cart. "Checking in."

Gia hugged her again. "All right, have a good flight."

"Thank you."

"We'll see you soon."

"You will," she promised, and turned to Elan. Caty bit her lip and nodded toward the door.

"Be there in a sec."

She headed toward the line of people approaching the gates. Elan turned to his sister.

She smiled. "Hand me the keys."

He fished them out of his pockets and did what he was told. "Hand me the *thing*."

"Give me a hug," she demanded, and he did. He felt his sister's hand slip into his jacket pocket.

"Nice." Elan chuckled, letting go of her.

"You need to put that in a bag; the sensors will ruin your surprise."

"Yes, I know. You should have put a note in here too, in case they insist," Elan joked.

"So? Propose on the spot; then you won't have to worry about hiding it," Gia said, her eyes widening.

"Can we give her some time to process? She's just moved out of her best friends' apartment to live with me, in Philly, by the way. I think we need to space things out."

"You're giving her time to change her mind," she joked. "Once she sees how you wash your clothes, she'll be out."

"I love you." Elan pulled her back in for a hug. "I'll call you when we land."

She hugged him back, shaking her head softly. "That'd be nice, but don't rush. And keep that box safe."

Elan nodded, sticking his hands into his pockets.

"Take care of each other," Gia said. "We'll be fine. We'll miss you, but we'll manage."

"I have no doubts."

He waved goodbye and went to join Caty.

"You ready?" she asked him, handing him his passport.

They made it through the gates and metal detectors, sensors included. She had no idea he was carrying a ring all the way to Philadelphia.

Seated next to each other on the plane, her hand reached over to his, her fingers caressing his palm before finding their place between his own. He squeezed her hand as she laid her head on his shoulder, looking out the window.

It had been a long wait, but it was fantastic to look back at how much they had grown. She was no longer watering plants; she was doing what she loved, had slowly started to work on bigger pieces and bigger spaces again. He had endured an arduous process of getting into the school of his choice, applying for funding, moving his entire life to a new place. There were a few dents in their time line that frustrated them both, but they never gave up.

"I love this part," she told him.

Elan closed his eyes and felt the ground move as the plane taxied faster. "Not scared?"

"Oh, I am." She held on to him tightly, her other hand joining their clasped hands. "But it's the good kind."

They both breathed out a sigh of relief as the wheels left the ground. They knew that after all the days of waiting, the long calls, and the wishful thinking—

They were finally taking off.

The End

AUTHOR'S NOTE

Stay a Little Longer is a product of a writing class held back
in 2016, hosted by #romanceclass and Mina V. Esguerra.
#romanceclass is a community of authors and readers who write
and read English-language romance books by Filipino authors.

I finished the manuscript when the class ended in 2017 but
chose to take my time in publishing it to work out its issues.
It has been over two years of going back and forth: wanting
to scrap it all and rooting for the story to be told. I am happy
to finally say that it is ready and that it has found its place at
Andrews McMeel Publishing at the right time.

The rest of the books that my friends wrote from the class are
now published under the #romanceclass Flair imprint. If you
wish to find out more about #romanceclass and adore stories
of happy ever afters, check out the website at:
www.romanceclassbooks.com.

WITH LOVE & GRATITUDE TO:

#romanceclass

Mina V. Esguerra

Layla Tanjutco, for the patience and for rooting for Caty and Elan.

Miles Tan

Jay E. Tria, for attending through multiple crises over this.

Inah, Jem, Kat, and Kate, for reading the very first drafts of this
book. Your comments gave me the confidence to keep working
on *Stay a Little Longer*.

Ilia and Maan

Patty Rice, Christine Schillig, and the rest of the Andrews McMeel
team. Thank you for the guidance, patience, and hard work.

To everyone who has read and loved my previous romance titles,
thank you for falling in love with the people I have created and
the stories that I told. I hope you love this one too.

To my family and my friends, who didn't know the full story
but have listened to me go on and on about my fictional-people
problems, thank you.

To J, the best friend I never met, thank you for the story.

Lastly, to you,
who could be waiting for the next call,
the next visit, the next embrace—
I hope this makes your wait a little bit more bearable.

Andrews McMeel Publishing
a division of Andrews McMeel Universal
1130 Walnut Street, Kansas City, Missouri 64106

www.andrewsmcmeel.com

19 20 21 22 23 LSC4 10 9 8 7 6 5 4 3 2 1

ISBN: 978-1-5248-5105-7

Library of Congress Control Number: 2018966162

Editor: Patty Rice
Art Director: Holly Swayne
Production Editor: Elizabeth A. Garcia
Production Manager: Carol Coe

ATTENTION: SCHOOLS AND BUSINESSES
Andrews McMeel books are available at quantity discounts with bulk purchase
for educational, business, or sales promotional use. For information, please
e-mail the Andrews McMeel Publishing Special Sales Department:
specialsales@amuniversal.com.